Misplaced Loyalty

RED BUD AVE
Publications
www.redbudave.com

Publisher's Note:
This is a work of fiction. Any names to historical events, real people, living and dead, or to real locales are intended only to give the fiction a setting in historic reality. Other names, characters, places, business and incidents are either the product of the author's imagination or are used fictitiously, and their resemblance, if any, to real life counterparts is entirely coincidental.

Library of Congress Catalog No.: Pending

ISBN 10: 0-9844397-4-9
ISBN 13: 978-0-9844397-4-4

Cover Design: Robert Ford, Jr.
Editor: Lea Mishell LeaMishellink@gmail.com
www.leanpub/b/TheLeaMishellCollection

FIRST EDITION

Printed in the United States of America

MISPLACED LOYALTY

TERESA SEALS

ACKNOWLEDGEMENTS

First and foremost, I want to thank God for the abundance of blessings I have received and all those yet to come.

When I first began to write and it came to this part, it came so easy for me to acknowledge those I felt worthy of the acknowledgments. I acknowledge nearly everyone that I encountered. Right now, although I have some very important people in my life, the only people that I want to acknowledge are my readers. Thank you for supporting my craft.

Also by Teresa Seals

Taylor Made

Simply Taylor Made

Washed Up

Diamonds Are Truly Forever

Tales From The Lou

Chapter 1

I'm Not a Kid Anymore

If I had no more time
No more time left to be here
Would you cherish what we had...

"Damn that's my shiiitt! I really hate I'm late. I'm gonna be late to my own damn funeral. Well, wedding cause I'm not about to say shit about not having no more time left to be here. 'Cause I still got shit to do here, but anyway I can't be on time for nothing. Visiting hours starts promptly at 2:15. It's 2:36." Angel had a little conversation with herself as she hopped out of her burgundy 2007 BMW *135i* Coupe. She made a mad dash to the entry of the jailhouse because it was now pouring down raining. Her attire, along with her hair pulled in her everyday ponytail, was perfect for this type of weather.

Walking up to the front desk, she laid her car keys down and took her ID out of her black velour Baby Phat jogging suit pocket.

"Who ya here to visit?" the shabby looking CO asked.

"Brooklin Johnson," Angel shot back looking at how tacky the blonde spiked extension ponytail looked as if it were lying like a rug on the CO's unrelaxed natural black hair. She tried to figure out why people wore the added-on ponytails without relaxing their own hair. That shit looked a hot mess. She thought to herself.

Pointing to the address book that looked like something from the sixties and the clipboard next to the outdated book, the CO said, "Put yo name and address here and over here the time, and the name of the offender ya here to see." Her overly manicured nails pointed at each location where the information was needed.

After instructing Angel, she turned around, the blonde spikes shaking vigorously as she spoke loudly. "Sorry, folks. We are so late starting Please form a single file line, wit' nothing in yo pockets, and if any gum in yo mouth, spit it out in dis here trash can," the shabby CO retorted as she pointed to the trash can next to the metal detector. The ponytail kept quivering as though it was ready to depart from her head.

Angel made it through the ancient looking metal door. There stood a longtime associate, Danita, in her CO uniform. "What have you been up to, Angel?"

"Shit!" said Angel, tooting her lips up as if she were smelling her top lip. "The same ole shit. I'm getting tired of running my ass down here to this motha fucking Jerk House. How Brooklin been holding up?"

Danita laughed at the Jerk House comment. The medium security facility, actually called the Workhouse, was simply a holdover that held inmates waiting on their court date before their sentencing. Being here you merely got jerked around.

Danita responded, "Being her. That girl ain't changed since high school. She's just doing her. How your fine ass brother doing? Now that's one dude that can get it!"

"Any who, I'll get back witcha later." Angel walked on through the door when the space permitted and the other visitors were clear of her way. She had no energy to talk about her brother Harlem.

Brooklin spotted Angel through the Plexiglas. Making hand gestures, signaling her to keep walking towards the end. Angel maneuvered her way through the maze and found a seat.

Both girls grabbed the phone at the same time, but Angel spoke first. "Don't be on all that crybaby bullshit. I'm not about to mess up my damn make-up fucking around with you. I had to hold my head down to run in here because I left my umbrella in the car and I didn't want my mascara to run!" She had to laugh at her own sarcasm.

"You don't even wear no motha fuckin' makeup, what are you talking 'bout? I ain't 'bout to cry anyway." Brooklin wiped the single tear from her right eye. "I'm just happy to see you. I do know one thing! I can't wait to get out this bitch! That public pretender is getting on my last nerve. That's a damn shame that at the beginning of the year I was out on the streets talking 'bout '07 is my year. Look at my ass now." Brooklin got that out with a slight bit of an annoyed sounding sigh.

Angel rolled her eyes trying to avoid the look of misery that was written all over her face. She hated to see her sister in this predicament. Brooklin always found herself in some type of mess, but the jail situation put the icing on the cake. Unaware of her older sister's innocence or guilt, she just sought after finding the middle ground. With this being Brooklin's first offense, all the jailhouse lawyers that they knew told them both that she could be released on her own recognizance and would probably receive papers for a couple of years. There was no evidence placing her at the scene of the crime. Basically, it all added up to don't waste the money.

With a secured bond set at $250,000, things didn't add up to Angel, but she listened to her older sister and didn't obtain a lawyer.

"How my kids?" Brooklin asked.

"Well, Denim talks too damn much and Brandon is slick as hell! Brandon ass needs some anger management. Those damn kids should be a damn billboard for birth control. I can see their picture big is day with a quote saying, *'This is what happens if you forget to take your birth control'*." Angel laughed thinking about the twins. "They remind me of you and Harlem when you all were little."

"Damn I only been here since July. It's just December. You acting like I been down for years!" Brooklin laughed, "And what you talking about when we were little? Girl, yo ass still little and I'll spank dat ass like I'd when we were kids! Don't get it twisted. You know what's up! Wit' yo wanna be Cinderella ass!"

They both shared a laugh thinking about how Angel was Cinderella crazy. Sometimes, she would ignore when she was called Angel. While they were trying to get her attention, she would prance and twirl around stating how Angel was "gone at the moment" and asked if "Cinderella" could help them.

"You betta gon' with that one too. You and Cinderella can kiss my ass. We ain't kids and I ain't little no mo. Play pussy if you want to."

"Play pussy and what?" Brooklin smirked with an angelic smile.

"Get fucked, that's what!"

Angel and Brooklin both shared another laugh.

"Any who, these five months seems like five years." Angel shook her head.

"Imagine how the fuck I feel. I ain't been dicked down in a hundred and fifty-one days." Brooklyn murmured, "As soon as I get out here I'm gonna find me a little duffle bag boy. Ya hear me."

Angel looked at Brooklin. "You got to be kidding me. That's why yo ass over there sitting with that orange state issued get-up on. Fucking with a damn duffle bag boy."

"Girl, my swag is like food stamps; niggas gotta have 'em. My life has always been ten percent sleep and ninety percent hustle. Money makes me cum," Brooklin chuckled and switched the subject. "Angel, answer me this."

Brooklin leaned into the Plexiglas making sure she had Angel's undivided attention. Angel rolled her eyes preparing for Brooklin's shenanigans.
"Do you believe in God?"

Angel nodded her head showing her approval in the question.

"Have you ever seen God?" Brooklin waited on her to answer.

Angel looked at Brooklin with disgust. "How can you play at a time like this? You better be asking Him for forgiveness! God is 'bout the only person who can save you right now."

Brooklin quickly changed the subject again. "You talked to Double R lately?"

"Yeah. He actually called this morning. Did I tell you he went up for parole October 25th. The day you go to court will make six weeks and he should've heard something by then."

"How long that nigga been down?"

"Brooklin, how old is your nephew?"

"Reggie is eleven. That's right! Double R got locked up when he was four months. Shit Double R got him a motha fucking ridah. You have been holding that nigga down for eleven years. I couldn't do it. I'd da told his ass the judge broke us up. See ya when I see ya. I don't see how Kevin puts up with your shit. Kevie-Kev is a good dude though."

"Kevin puts up with my ass cuz I fulfill all of his fantasies. You know shawty right here is the shit!" Angel pointed to herself as she sang the short tune. "How long is this visit?"

"Why you ask that every time you come here?" Brooklin asked a tad bit aggravated.

"Because they either start sooner than they supposed to or end later than they supposed to. Shit, these damn raunchy ass CO's down here set they own visiting schedule. It ain't shit like going to see Reggie. Them crackers start on time and end on time."

"When was the last time you been to see him?" Brooklin asked.

Angel refused to answer. She didn't want Brooklin to think that if she got some time she would slow up on the visits.

For the first four years, Angel drove for two hours to see Reggie every weekend faithfully. Sometimes she would rent a room so that she would get to visit the entire weekend. When Kevin came into the picture seven years ago, things began to slightly change. Throughout the years, Angel's visits became sporadic with Reggie. She attempted to send cards weekly. Angel saw to it that he got pictures and letters at least once a month.

"Well, I'm not going to be here next Sunday, so I will come see you on Tuesday." Angel informed her sister.

"What you got up?" Brooklin inquired.

"I'm going out of town with Teresa."

"Who is Teresa?"

"You know my crony Teresa Seals that wrote that book *Taylor Made*."

"Where y'all going and what are y'all going for?" Brooklin asked with sarcasm and some slightness of jealousy in her voice.

"We are going to New Jersey. She is hooking up with some cat that has started his own publishing company."

"Who?" Brooklin inquired.

"I can't think of his name, but he has some big things planned for his company. He has ghostwritten for a few people, and he supposed to be some kin to 50 Cent."

"That's what's up! You started on your book

yet?"

"I haven't quite healed yet. I'm not trying to open that wound just yet. Know what I mean?" Angel choked up thinking about the story she had to tell. "I'm going to bring the kids with me when I come back." Angel stopped talking as she watched the CO speak to her sister.

"That's your sister?" the CO asked Brooklin.

"Yep!" Brooklin spoke proudly.

"Y'all look just alike. She's just a little lighter than you. Where did she get them grey eyes from?"

"Actually they change colors. My brother and I use to call her a cat. During the winter, they are grey and in the warmer time of the year, they are hazel like mine. Our daddy had all kind of shit mixed up in him, but our mommy was a black stallion!" Brooklin nodded her head up and down.

Brooklin noticed Angel becoming annoyed so she cut her conversation short with the CO.

"She was just telling me that I have ten minutes left. Do you have money on you?"

"Why?" Angel asked.

"I want you to put some money on my books."

"You sound just like a nigga. Put some money on my books." Angel laughed grabbing her crotch as if she were a dude.

"Fuck you! Do you have some damn money or what?"

"Yes. I'll put a bill fifty on your books. Does that machine charge you for using it?"

"Yeah. I think its three dollars. So that will leave me with a hundred forty-seven dollars." Brooklin made hand motions to make sure her figures were accurate, "Love ya lil' sis. Tell the boys I am going to call them later on tonight."

Brooklin waited for Angel to say her love you's and they both hung up the phone. Both departing the visiting area and proceeding to their destinations, Angel arrived at the machine as she inserted the money she had stuck in her bra.

Chapter 2

BACK IN THE DAY

"Brooklin, Harlem, and Angeeeeel!" Luther yelled for his children holding the broken screen door. From the front of the apartment, he could see the playground that was adjacent to the housing project. Immediately, they stopped playing and ran to see what their father wanted. Angel ran the slowest because she had on her plastic Cinderella heels. She was holding her Tiara with one hand and her magic wand with the other.

Running in the house as usual, they all tried to grab a body part and tugged away at him asking if they could stay out a little longer. His kids had a way with him. Sometimes he would allow them to stay out longer or he we just go out there to supervise their activities.

Luther and his family resided in Carr Square Village housing project. Carr Square Village, a low-rise development built in 1942 to house low-income blacks, it consisted of row homes in front of the five high-rise projects called the Vaughn Family Apartments. All of it in a nutshell was the *projects*.

Luther's top priority were his children then his wife. His wife's needs never went unmet; she simply knew where she stood. It was so evident that his children came first. When they all were just babies, she never had to get up in the middle of the night. He took care of that. That was his bonding time.

He worked part-time at a lumberyard near the housing project. He was paid under the table so it wouldn't interfere with his disability check. He did other side hustles just to bring in extra money. His wife, Brenda, was the homemaker. Her job was to take care of home and keep an eye on the children when Luther was away.

Born and raised in New York, Luther was a Vietnam vet who met up with some guys from St. Louis, MO during 'Nam. Due to a slipped disc in his back, he received his Honorable Discharge in 1972. He was raised by his grandmother who died while he was away in 'Nam. Luther's mother only lived two hours after she had given birth to him and all he knew about his father was that his name was Harlem. He didn't know whether it was his real name or his street name. The way his grandmother ran it down to him, his very own mother may not have known the sperm donor's name. According to his grandmother, it may have been in Harlem where he was conceived.

Luther could pass for Asian as long as he kept his hair cut low and didn't open his mouth. He stood five foot five with a pale complexion. He had a slight resemblance to Arnold Horshack from the old TV sitcom, "Welcome Back, Kotter", especially by the hair. All of his children inherited that wild black brown curly hair. Luther's grandmother was a Puerto Rican. Being that she never mentioned a grandfather, it appeared to him that the apple didn't fall to far from the tree. His mother didn't take after her mother at all when it came to looks. She was a beautiful dark chocolate complexion with long luxurious coal black hair. He would carry his one and only picture of her in his wallet. The picture was kept in perfect condition. He took good care of it.

When he came home from the war, he went to the only place that he knew was home: Flatbush Garden projects in Brooklyn, New York. When he made it to the ninth floor and knocked on the door, a new family was residing there. He was stunned to see the family at first because while growing up, no one ever came to visit. They knew exactly who he was. The current residents who invaded his home had been opening the mail he was sending to his grandmother. The family informed him that she had passed a year ago and they attempted to write him but he never had a return address. They went on to let him know that she had a nice service. An old male friend took special care of the service. Luther was able to leave with a pleasing feeling.

Luther headed to visit the place where the family stated his grandmother was buried. With some instructions, he was able to visit the gravesite. He walked over and told his grandmother his final goodbyes.

He left New York by the way of train. When he reached St. Louis, he stopped to get a bite to eat at a small bar and grill across from the train station and that's when he saw her. Blinking his eyes, he squinted to make out the image he was seeing. He thought he was seeing things. He did several double takes. What he saw was a spitting image of his mother. The only difference was she wore an afro. Luther approached her instantly.

Brenda had just arrived in St. Louis. In minutes of their conversation, Luther found out that Brenda's mother sent her to St. Louis. They lived in a whorehouse in Henderson, Kentucky. A couple of the johns were approaching her but Brenda's mother had other plans for her daughter. Now that she had turned eighteen, her mother sent her to St. Louis to get established with plans on joining her daughter later.

When he touched Brenda, he felt the tenderness of her skin. "Tenda Brenda" was the pet name he had given her. To him, she was tender as the winter breeze. Nine months later, Luther and Brenda gave birth to their first child, Brooklin. Luther chose the name in remembrance of the borough where he grew up. A year later, they had his first and only son. He chose the name Harlem in reference to the father he never met. He didn't want him to be a junior because he felt he needed his own identity.

It had been three years since a baby had been in the house when Angel was born. Brenda's aunt called her when she was six months pregnant to tell her that her mother had been killed. As she listened to the details, Brenda began to receive some abdominal pain. Brenda's aunt informed her that no one had seen her since Saturday. She assumed that she had made it to St. Louis because she'd tell everyone, "You gonna look up and I'm ma be gone to sweet St. Louie." Her mother would say angelically.

Brenda's mother was found buried in the snow on the same street she lived and worked. Six houses down from the whorehouse. No one saw or heard anything. Brenda asked about the arrangements. Rumors surfaced that Brenda's alleged father was behind the death, but he was never questioned. Those in charge of the case found it not to be of any importance. Just another prostitute dead was the attitude that the laws had taken on with the case.

An hour after hanging up with her aunt, she gave birth to the couple's third child. She felt this was a supernatural being she had given birth to. Usually at 24 weeks, the blood vessels in the lungs are still developing. Her child weighed five pounds even and was fully developed. Brenda always believed that angels were messengers from God. When she laid eyes on her baby, she felt she had seen an extraordinary beauty. To add to that, she was born on her mother's birthday, November 22nd. Being that angels are described as pure and bright as Heaven, consequently, she believed she was holding her angel. Brenda definitely wasn't letting Luther name their child after another borough in New York, so she named her gift, Angel. Luther didn't contend. He kissed the forehead of his child and whispered, "Daddy's messiah."

Luther was proud of his family. Having every intention of being that rock that kept his family together and giving his children something he never had, he took pride in his family as he adored his beautiful children. Brooklin resembled his mother and wife, and Angel favored him, except she possessed a mysterious eye color. Harlem was a mixture of both of his parents. His complexion was blended caramel peach. His skin was as soft as a baby's bottom. His hair was coal black with thick curly locks. He nose was perfectly proportioned along with his lips. Together they resembled every ounce of ethnicity they had inherited; they were truly a taste of the rainbow.

Brooklin, Harlem, and Angel grew up not knowing they were poor. Luther and Brenda provided to the utmost. It was good until the late eighties when things went downhill. Nancy Reagan was blasted everywhere with the slogan JUST SAY NO, and Luther began running around saying YES.

Luther had taken his children to the theatre to see *Krush Groove*. He dropped them off not even waiting to see if they had made it in. In 1986, New

Edition was losing Bobby Brown and Brenda was losing Luther. Odds and ends were coming up missing. Brenda knew the problem, but keeping her family together was most important. Strange people came by looking for Luther and his appearance around the house came to a minimum until he didn't appear at all.

The girls didn't understand what had happened to their father but Harlem knew. Luther gave him the talk on how he had this monkey on his back and he was now the man of the house. He told Harlem he needed to take care of home because he was no longer capable and promised he'd return once he got himself together. At that time, Harlem didn't understand but he grew to understand. He made a promise never to go the route of the older guys from the housing project. He saw all the flashy cars and jewelry, but he knew the same way they got those things destroyed his home.

Through a temp agency, Brenda landed a permanent position as the secretary to the President and CEO of Bi-State Transit Agency. Bi-State owns and operates the St. Louis Metropolitan region's public transportation system. After five years on the job, Brenda was able to move her family from the projects to the city's outskirts of the Central West End. The Central West End is a diverse community in mid St. Louis. The area consists of a fine balance of businesses, homeowners, and renters. It also has a fine balance of homosexuals.

Brenda's boss was selling his family home. His parents were moving into a retirement home. Most homes in that area went for at least two hundred thousand. She barely paid a fourth of that. Maybe because of the overtime she was putting in and the admiration from her boss.

Their house was enormous. The prior family was able to raise eight children there. The house was over one hundred years old. It was a beautiful three-story, ten room home with wonderful original millwork, pocket doors, wood floors, built-in cabinetry, four fireplaces with gorgeous mantles, some antique lighting, as well as a large two car garage and fenced-in backyard. The four bedrooms, each with a private bath, plus a 32' x 16' master bedroom suite with adjoining master bath complete with a Jacuzzi tub. The updated kitchen included a marble island and adjacent butler's pantry. Unlike many older homes, there was abundant storage space with walk-in closets in every room.

The Johnson family instantly fell in love with their new home. As a housewarming gift, the house was fully furnished with new furniture. Brenda quickly enforced the "don't ask, don't tell" policy.

Brenda informed her boss that she would never allow her children to see her with another man. Therefore, he got a condo out in Ladue, an affluent area whose median household income ranged from $200,000 to $350,000.

"Hello!" Angel said as she paused and listened to the operator tell her she had a collect call. After listening to the instructions, she pressed five.

"Yeah, yeah, yeah! What y'all doing?" Brooklin asked.

"We are getting ready for the funeral," Angel responded looking into the mirror brushing on some rouge.

"Damn! Who dun died now!?" Brooklin asked thinking they were just at their mother's funeral around this time last year.

"You know Nikki's aunt, Auntie," Angel confirmed trying to hold back her tears.

"I hate to hear that. How Joe-Joe holding up?"

Brooklin asked, thinking about her first love.

"I don't know. I haven't seen him since he has been home from the Air Force."

"Well, tell everybody I said hey. I'll call y'all when I think y'all back home. Love ya." Brooklin hung up before Angel could respond.

Brooklin walked away from the payphone thinking of all the inevitable. She didn't hear anything no one was saying. She made it to her cell and fell into a deep slump. Lowering her head to miss the top bunk, she lay down and drifted off to sleep.

Angel held back all her tears. Not really being ready to attend another funeral, and not wanting the boys to see her cry, she thought about some good things.

"Here comes Salt-n-motha fucking-Pepa. The two most gorgeous women in the whole wide hood." Angel laughed at Boogey the wino that appeared to have a permanent residence in front of the liquor store as he did his rendition of Salt-n-Pepa's "Push It." The old players from around the way had given him the name Boogey because he was always singing and dancing. Angel laughed thinking of the good ole days.

Angel continued to reminisce.

"Angel and Harlem let's go outside and meet the neighbors." Brooklin yelled to the top of the stairs as she turned and walked up to the door with her siblings in tow.

To the left of them was the Davis family. Nikky and her four brothers: Joe-Joe, Brian, Robbie, and Rodney, lived next door with their aunt Auntie and their cousin Nita. Auntie was the mother of the neighborhood. Her front door was like a lazy Susan. People were constantly going in and out. Nothing illegal went on there. She was one of those types that if everybody is here, I know that everybody is okay.

A door down from the Davis family were the Clarks. Keith, Kevin, Kenneth, and Keisha. They lived with their mother Pee-Wee.

Across the street were four more households with children. There was Toni, who lived with her aunt and uncle.

Next door to Toni were the Dixons. The Dixons kept their grandchildren, Ruth and Rachel, on the weekends and the girls were there all summer long.

Next door to the Dixons were Tim, Chad, and Terrell Miller. They were the only kids that lived in a two parent home.

Then there was Lil Charles. He was the youngest of six children. His mother worked at a tavern. She was never home at night and all of his siblings were grown and out on their own. So of course his house was the hot spot.

Down the street were the toughest kids on the block. The McClendon's: Earl, Quincy, Ulysses, Paul and Tyrone. Big Shirley had to be equipped with a metal heart just to love those boys. They weren't ugly boys. They were just bad as hell. The neighborhood terrorists, breaking and entering, riding in stolen cars and defacing property were all notches on their belts. Tyrone was cold with his hands. They were knocking niggas out in five seconds flat. He was the neighborhoods Mike Tyson.

Their block had two Caucasian families. They weren't seen much. They used their back doors. Both families were childless. The families lived on separate ends of the block. The rest of the families either had no children or they were the ages of Lil' Charles' older siblings.

As you can see, the boys on the block outnumbered the girls. So the girls had no other choice but to play what they played. How does the saying go, when in Rome one must do as the Romans. Brooklin, Angel, Keisha, Toni, and Rachel found themselves being in Rome. Ruth, Nikki, and Nita were a tad bit older. They were into boys with toys. The toys consisted of money and cars. So they were not really part of the family.

Everyone else hung out tight. From racing in the street with no shoes on, playing stick ball, football, boxing, and nigga knocking. The nigga knocking was the funniest of all. That quickly ended when one night Quincy McClendon walked up on the white man's porch. Mr. Whitey stood tall with pistol in hand. Everyone stood in amazement. Mr. Whitey said nothing at all. Quincy backed away so quick. Everybody talked about what they would have done had that been them. That night led to Joe-Joe and Brooklin's little love affair.

The family was all sitting on Joe-Joe's porch when the game of "Truth or Dare" got kicked off. No one had feelings for anyone. The guys looked upon the girls as if they were one of the guys. That was until Earl dared Joe-Joe to tongue kiss Brooklin for two minutes. They walked to the gangway. The gangway was pitch black except for the lights barely extending from the house across from it.

Joe-Joe and Brooklin stood up under the window and kissed for more than two minutes. When they finally came back, no one said anything. Angel looked at her sister with disgust, not believing that she had kissed the four-eyed neighbor. Everyone sat quietly until the Miller's porch light came on. That was the cue that the curfew for everyone was slowly approaching.

Joe-Joe and Brooklin's love affair lasted until a new kid moved on the block then Joe-Joe was kicked totally to the curb.

Vincent Jackson was the new kid on the block. He was from Decatur, IL. Vincent moved in with some relatives two houses away from the McClendon's.

No one knows how the two hooked up but it happened. Joe-Joe didn't have a problem with the new item at all. He and Vincent became the best of friends.

Harlem bowed out. When Vincent came in the picture, he stopped hanging out. Harlem didn't like the vibe he received from Vincent. Instead, he connected with his books.

Although Brooklin was older than him by a few months, she and Harlem were in the same grade. Brooklin had a late birthday and Harlem's birthday was within the guidelines to register him into kindergarten the same year. Usually the sister outshines the boy, but not in this case. Harlem ran circles around Brooklin when it came to the books. Harlem got that from his mother. Brooklin was a fast talker and slick with the tongue, beauty but no brains. While Brooklin was out having her fun, Harlem was in the house doing their homework.

Chapter 3

LET'S GET IT STARTED

"Five, four, three, two, one. Happy New Year!" Everyone yelled wearing his or her 1988 party hats. The whole block was in Auntie's basement. She let Nikki throw a New Year's party. Soon after everybody brought in the New Year, they started to depart and go home. Parents agreed that the children could stay over at Auntie's.

Dispersing to their respective places, Vincent walked Brooklin home. Harlem pushed Angel in the door as he waited for Brooklin.

Vincent was about to push up on Brooklin until he saw the look Harlem was giving him. Brooklin turned to see what had Vincent shook. When she saw Harlem, she said her goodbyes. They all turned in for the night.

"Y'all need to hurry up. The bus is coming at 1:30!" Harlem yelled to his sisters. Harlem acted more like 33 instead of the thirteen year old child he was. His voice was also changing. It was getting deeper. His puny body started to transform. Within a year, his body resembled the model Tyson Beckford.

They ran to catch their bus. Just as they were

approaching the stop, the bus was pulling up. They got to Union Station ten minutes before the movie they came to see started. As they made it inside, Harlem rushed to purchase their tickets. He handed the girls their tickets and proceeded to take his seat. Angel and Brooklin went straight to the concession line to purchase some popcorn and drinks. When they made it to the designated area, "Colors" was just beginning. Brooklin fell in love with Don Cheadle's character, "Rocket."

After the movie ended, Harlem walked out saying, "Everybody and they momma is going to be in some type of gang after seeing this shit!"

As soon as they made it to the bus stop, some dudes that had "Laclede Town Thunder Catz" airbrushed on their t-shirts were yelling Hoova Deuce.

Harlem looked at his sisters and shook his head. That's when Reggie walked up to Angel. "Aren't you in my class?"

Angel blushed and nodded her head up and down. Harlem thought that he was going to have to get busy with this dude for talking to his ten-year-old sister. When he noticed he wasn't wearing one of those shirts and looked to be the same age as Angel, he believed the conversation was innocent.

Things happened so fast. This high yellow chic with a Jheri curl named Tammy standing with a group of girls yelled out, "I'll beat that bitch ass!"

Brooklin had been having problems with Tammy at school but she never acted upon them. Brooklin didn't know what type of problems Tammy had with her. Brooklin turned to her, looking her up and down in her Palmetto jeans and Spuds McKenzie T-Shirt. Tammy kind of favored the dog on her shirt. Brooklin barked, "Don't talk about it, bitch be about it!"

Harlem looked at Brooklin and spoke calmly,

"You betta whoop her ass because if you don't, you are going to have to deal with me."

Brooklin walked over to Tammy with Harlem and Angel following behind her. Harlem spoke aggressively to the group. "This is a one on one!" He stood back and put his hand in his pocket. In a matter of five minutes, Brooklin literally dog walked Tammy. Tammy didn't get one lick in, she was covering her face the entire time. They never had another problem.

Brooklin walked back over to her siblings and looked at them directly. "Just like you believe in God, you need to believe in me!"

Harlem and Angel looked at each other with confusion. Brooklin walked off and they followed behind.

Angel thought about Reggie all day. She couldn't wait until Monday morning rolled around. Angel slid into her Gloria Vanderbilt jeans, white oxford, white thick IZOD socks and brown penny loafers with the penny in the slot. She was up bright and early. When she made it to school, she was so happy to see Reggie. She got a little disappointed when she saw him come to class with his shirt reppin' "Blue Bud Crips." She instantly thought about her brother's comments and the ending of the movie "Colors." No one seemed to walk away alive. Her puppy love was over as soon as it began, for now anyway. She was oblivious to the fact that she had met one of the most malicious hood figures ever assembled in the making.

Brooklin, on the other hand, had a whole other perception. She was in search of her "Rocket." She soon found him. His name was Cordell, better known to the hood as Casper. He received this name because no one happens to see him coming or going. Having friendly characteristics wouldn't fly for long; he later became known as C-Note as his money game increased. His hood was clicked up tight. They claimed either "87 Kitchen Crip" or "Six Deuce." Those boys went by some crazy names: Stretch, Playa, Flintstone, Sweet Pea, Highlife, B. K., Scooley, Trippa, and Slick. The only somebody that had a name to fit was this cat named Face. The crew started calling him Scarface because his face on the left side was fucked. A car they stole ran hot and his smart ass took the radiator top off. He survived but he wasn't any Scarface so they shortened it to Face. These cats went around wearing orange and brown with brown San Diego baseball caps in reference to the set they claimed, "Six Deuce," as they went around the hood yelling, "N Hood!" College and Carter, later shortened to CNC, is where these cats could be found.

Just like Joe-Joe, Brooklin kicked Vincent to the curb. He was persistent though. Vincent called every day. He'd sit on Joe-Joe's porch to wait on Brooklin to come out or go in.

Brooklin was never mean to him. She talked to Vincent as if he was Harlem. Vincent was the one and only person that listened to Brooklin when she compared herself to the high power. She convinced him when she asked, "You see me every day. You ain't ever seen him, so why wouldn't you believe in me?"

Vincent felt as though he had lost his friend. Brooklin was the only one who had accepted him. Everybody was doing their own thing.

The McClendon boys had stepped into a whole other playing field. Big Shirley had taken ill. She was still getting around, but not like she used to.

The oldest boy, Earl, stepped up to the plate. He hooked up with some cat name K-Rock that had the Lou on lock. Everybody that sold crack comped from him. Earl was K-Rock's right hand. Quincy, Ulysses, Tyrone, and Paul were equipped to bring the heat if they had any problems in the street.

The Mac Boys were bringing the heat. Everyone rolled around in their short dog Cadillac's.

Ruth and Rachel left the block in hopes of becoming actresses while Kenneth, Keith, and Kevin left Keisha to become R&B singers. They started a group called "K-LUV" and were finished before they got started.

Toni and Lil Charles became an item. They were the first casualties of teenage pregnancy on the block. It seemed as soon as they got together, Toni was pregnant. Nikki was soon to follow. Tyrone and Paul were both doing her so she didn't know which McClendon fathered her child.

The close knit family structure of the block had suddenly taken a turn for the worst. Days went by where friends barely saw each other. The hang out spot was no longer at Auntie's. This was the beginning of the loyalty becoming misplaced.

Brenda was on her way out the house. As she was about to leave out the door, she paused, standing there trying to figure out why was there a shadow on the porch when everyone was gone to school. She opened the door slowly, looking down at the shadow. "Vincent! Boy you scared me! Why aren't you at school?"

Vincent uttered, "Mrs. Johnson, I'm sorry if I scared you. I was waiting to talk to Brooklin."

After locking the door and securing it, Brenda looked at Vincent. "Is there something I can help you with?"

Vincent nodded his head yes. "Brooklin dun jumped off my dick and now she's on the next nigga dick and I'm hurting."

Brenda looked at Vincent slightly confused. She didn't know whether to slap him for disrespecting her or hug him because she could see the hurt in his eyes as well as hear it in his voice.

"Vincent, all I can say is if you love something, let it go. If it comes back, it is meant to be yours and if it doesn't, you will never know. Let me tell you this. The man in Brooklin's life walked out the door and never came back. We all were affected by it but we all handled it differently. She cried every night praying he would come back. She stills cries and prays he will come back. Her father disappointed her. I disappointed her because she believed that I should have gone looking for him and brought him home. Right now, she's looking to be loved. It's not the love I can give her. She's looking for that fatherly love she once had. Once she thinks she's found it, before there's any disappointment, she does what she believes is best and that's to walk away. I'm not saying that it's right. Hell, I might not be right. She'll come around." Brenda brought the conversation to an end as she hugged Vincent and walked off the porch.

Vincent watched Brenda as she got in her car and she drove down the street before disappearing into the sunset. His thoughts ran away with Brenda as she drove off.

"Vincent! Vincent! Dude do you hear me?" Earl yelled as he pulled up in his white short dog caddy pimped out with Trues and Vogues.

Vincent shook his head from his thoughts. "Damn dude how long you been right there?"

Earl shook his head in disbelief. "I just pulled up. What's wrong with you? You acting as if you just seen a ghost?"

Vincent walked over to the car and got in. "Where you about to go to?"

Earl chuckled, "I'm on a paper chase."

Vincent looked him dead in his eyes. "I'm rolling with you."

Thinkin' of a master plan
'Cause ain't nuthin' but sweat inside my hand...

Earl and Vincent rolled out blasting Eric B. and Rakim. Vincent didn't know this ride would be the point of no return.

Chapter 4

LOVE DON'T LIVE HERE ANYMORE

Everybody that was anybody was at the Checkerdome in mid-August for the "Fresh Fest Tour" to see Run-DMC, Whodini, Public Enemy, EPMD, Jazzy Jeff and the Fresh Prince, and JJ Fad.

Harlem stepped in the place in his black and white shell toe Adidas with no shoestrings in them, black Levi jeans, black and white Adidas jacket, and black Kangol hat with the white kangaroo.

Brooklin sported black stirrups, purple leg warmers, a purple oxford, and purple white girl canvas tennis shoes. The leg warmers were worn to make a fashion statement, not to keep the legs warm. Up her arm was an array of purple and black friendship bracelets. The simple bracelets merely represented nothing back in the day but nowadays they relate to how people get down sexually.

Angel went for a more subtle look as she chose her Jordache blue jeans with her platinum name belt with ANGEL in bold letters across her waist, a red Coca-Cola sweatshirt, and red leather Fila tennis shoes.

Brooklin had to take a double look when she saw Vincent taking pictures with Earl and his posse. Vincent was posing in his blue Adidas jogging suit wearing a very big gold rope. When she looked to his hands he had a wad of money holding it up as if he were bidding his hand in a card game.

She had a little taste of what the rapper Biz Markie called vapors, becoming infatuated with money Vincent was holding. When she last saw him, he had on some Wrangler jeans, a Paisley shirt and some XJ900's from PayLess.

C-Note's appearance removed her from her vapors zone. He approached them with his crew and a look of disgust grew upon Harlem's face. Angel was holding a conversation about nothing to distract her brother from focusing on Brooklin. Reggie came up and spoke to Angel and Harlem. Harlem's demeanor had a slight change realizing that Reggie's presence was purely innocent until a slew of guys walked up over to C-Note and Reggie to join them. Harlem wanted to go into attack mode but, with better judgment, he laid back as Angel stood by his side sensing his rage. She stroked his ego and put him at ease as she called out to Brooklin to inform her that the intermission was just about over and they needed to head back to their seats.

As they walked back towards the corridor to their seats, Vincent walked up. "What up Harlem!" He reached out to embrace him. Harlem slightly hesitated, but eventually obliged when he noticed Vincent acted as if he didn't see Brooklin.

Everything was interrupted as echoes began to say…

Relax your mind, let your conscience
Be free and get to the sounds of EPMD

Everyone ran towards their seats reciting the lyrics to the song. Vincent stood in the background as he watched Brooklin do the Wop and the Cabbage Patch as she found her seat.

When the concert ended, people that were capable to drive off did and those that needed to wait went to their respective areas and waited for their rides to arrive. Brooklin, Harlem, and Angel's mother told them to meet her at Imo's up on Oakland. Heading to their destination was a crowd of guys rapping the lyrics to a few of the artist that hit the stage. Harlem searched the crowd to get a photogenic copy of the faces just in case he needed them for later. He laid his eyes directly on C-Note.

He grabbed Brooklin's arm. "Look here! That dude has bad news written all over his ass. Say whatcha gotta say to him and let's go up here to Imo's and wait on Momma. Make it snappy Brooklin!" Harlem spoke with aggression in his voice. His soft skin tone had become flushed with frustration.

Angel stood beside her big brother looking like a sad puppy dog. The look wasn't because something was wrong; it was to make her innocence known. He hadn't realized Angel stood there beside him on point and if anybody said anything to him out of line, she was going for crown to hold her big brother down.

Brooklin walked up to C-Note standing there in the midst of his crowd of friends. "I see you travel with an entourage. Who are all these people with you?"

He turned around to point to each individual. "Well, this is Stretch with his tall ass, Playa and all the ladies love him, Flintstone, Sweet Pea, B. K., Scooley, Trippa, Slick, and Face. That's Ducky, Brownie, and T-Bone. These my boys from my hood. Right there are my boys that are from the Red Bud. That's No Brains," he said pointing to a short Ice Cube looking cat. "You already know the lil' dude Double R. He be trying to get up with your little sister." He continued to point. "Lay-Loc, Six-Loc, Peep Dog, D.A., Scary, Cent Dog, Baddie, Clack 'cause he click clack those bangers and that's his brother Nine, and dude standing back there black as a motha fucka is Midnight." Midnight stood there looking like T-Pain without the dreads.

Brooklin frowned. "What type of names are those? What y'all think y'all some gangsters."

C-Note smiled. "We money makers. The names just describe their character. For instance, take my man Cent Dog. He carries a bunch of change. Every time he pays for something he pays with change."

Brooklin shook her head listening to what she thought was pure nonsense but it turned her on at the same time. "That dude looks just like a damn duck with freckles."

C-Note laughed. "That's why we call his yellow ass Ducky."

"Well, what does B. K. and D.A. stand for?"

"Byron King and Derrick Adams!" C-Note spoke proudly of his crew.

"Well, Cordell I will talk to you later." Brooklin kissed him on the cheek and ran off to catch up with Harlem and Angel.

As she approached them, Brenda was pulling up in her blue two door Cougar. Harlem opened the door and held the seat so that the girls could get in the back. Harlem got in and shut the door.

Looking over at Harlem, Brenda asked, "How was the concert?"

"It was cool. Can we get some White Castle's?" Harlem looked over at his mother.

"Momma cut that up!" Angel screamed and started to sing *Supersonic*.

By the time the song ended, they had made it to White Castle. Entering the inside, Angel laid eyes directly on Luther. He was sitting over in the booth with three other grimy looking men. "Daddy!" she screamed and ran over him giving him the tightest clinch ever. Tears filled her eyes. She ignored the stench of piss reaping from him.

Luther smiled. "There goes my little messiah. How has daddy's baby girl been?"

She caught him up on everything from the new house to the concert which they had just left. Luther walked up to Brenda. "Tenda Brenda, you still look as beautiful as the day I met you in that train station."

Brenda looked him over from head to toe. With an innocent smile, she spoke to him with an unconcerned tone. "I wish I could say the same."

"Hey Harlem and Brooklin." He reached out to give them a hug. Brooklin refused as she frowned upon the smell.

Harlem shook his hand. "What's going on, daddy?"

Brooklin looked at him with disgust and rolled her eyes commencing to ignore his presence.

Luther was crushed from Brooklin's actions as he answered Harlem's question. "Struggling to stay above water, that's all."

He altered himself heading in the way in which he came. As he walked away heading in the direction of his friends who had watched everything taking place, Angel ran up to him and handed him the receipt from their order. "Daddy calls us sometime. No matter what you have done, you are still our father. We still love you." The sadness was so evident in her voice.

He turned and said, "Better yet, let me use your ink pen." He tore the receipt in half.

Angel looked in her blue jean Gitano purse and pulled out the requested item. Luther scribbled on the paper. "Here why don't we call each other?"

Angel grinned, "I can do that." She turned to walk out the door when she noticed everyone she came with had left out. When she reached the door, she looked back, with the look of not wanting to leave her father. "I love you daddy." Everyone in White Castle turned to stare at Luther, watching this heartfelt moment.

Luther's friends put their heads down filled with shame. They too had a family they had left in despair. Luther blew her a kiss. Angel reached her hand up to catch it, placed the kiss within her hand, and she walked out the door.

As soon as she made it home, Angel ran to the telephone. She pulled the number from her back pocket and began to dial the number her father had given her. Disappointment quickly fell upon her as she heard the operator say, "I'm sorry the number you have dialed has been disconnected. Please hang up and try your call again."

Chapter 5

JUST ME AND YOU

Angel sat in her room constantly pushing pause from play and play to pause buttons on her double cassette big black boom box. She was sitting down writing the lyrics to Eazy E's song *The Boyz in the Hood*. Harlem and Brooklin were getting ready to head to the mall to shop for some outfits for their eighth grade graduation.

Brenda walked into Angel's room. "Angel, do you want to go to the mall with us?"

"No. I am going to stay here by myself and enjoy being home alone," Angel smiled at her mother.

"Okay baby. Do you want anything?" Brenda inquired.

"Just bring me something back to eat. Something like some butter pecan ice cream," Angel smiled.

"You gotta eat more than some damn ice cream. You are little enough. Somebody would think I don't feed you. You need to eat something to get some meat on them bones," Brenda laughed as she walked out the room and shut the door.

Ten minutes after they had left the house, the phone rang. "Hello," Angel spoke holding the receiver up to her ear.

"Speak to, Angel," the male voice uttered.

"Who dis?" Angel asked wondering what boy would be calling her. She had never given anyone her phone number, neither classmates nor the people she associated with in the neighborhood. The neighbors simply came to knock on the door if they wanted anything. This call caught her by surprise. Her mother never gave her permission to talk to boys on the phone. She didn't say she could and neither did she say she couldn't.

"This Double R. I mean, it's Reggie."

"Oh hi, Reggie," Angel said, confused about what he wanted and wondering how he got the number.

"Brooklin gave me the number."

"And why would she do that?" Speaking with an attitude, Angel did the snake with her neck.

"Because, I asked her for it," Reggie aggressively answered.

"Why did you ask her for it?" Angel's attitude was still present.

"Because I wanted to talk to you." Reggie wanted to end the sentence with dummy but he decided against it.

"And what do you want to talk to me about?"

"Do you want to go to the movies with me?" Reggie was not giving up no matter how much attitude she was giving him.

"I don't know. Give me some time to think about it. Plus, I need to ask my mother. I don't think I'm allowed to go out with boys yet," Angel whispered very nonchalantly.

"What are you doing?" he asked not wanting to get off the phone.

"I'm writing a song down." Angel looked down at the line paper looking over the words to the song.

"You were making up your own song?"

"No. I am writing Eazy E's song down."

"You like rap music?" Reggie began to think of

anything to make conversation. He had recently seen her at the concert so he knew she had to be a fan.

"Do I like rap music? I LOVE rap music!" Angel couldn't believe he asked such a silly question. She rolled her eyes as if he could see her attitude.

"I thought you would be all in love with some New Edition, Full Force, Ready for the World, Force MD's, and Troop type of shit," Reggie laughed.

"I do like all that, but I'd rather listen to rap. Speaking of rap, do people tell you that you look just like Jam Master Jay from Run-DMC?"

Reggie laughed, "Everybody says that. I wish I had money like Jam Master Jay."

"Any thang's possible." Angel turned her pitch to a hip-hop tone. "All you gotta do is put your mind to it and through Christ you can accomplish whatever. Nothing comes to a dreamer but a dream."

"I heard that. What do you wanna be when you grow up?" Reggie felt Angel had just schooled him and that was his only comeback.

"All that I can be!" Angel spoke proudly.

"You wanna go to the Army?" Reggie asked.

"Hell naw!" Angel retorted.

They both chuckled.

"You wanna hear something?"

"Hear what?" Angel asked.

Reggie rumbled through all of his cassette tapes. He found exactly what he was looking for. Reggie put his tape in his boom box and pushed play as Kool Moe Dee's voice poured through the speakers asking his listeners *How Ya Like Me Now*.

"That ain't nothing." Angel pulled out her music and blasted some Boogie Down Productions and let him know about being blinded as KRS-One talked about *Criminal Minded*.

They went back and forth playing everything from MC Lyte, Just Ice, Audio Two, Doug E. Fresh,

Slick Rick, LL Cool J, Dana Dane, Big Daddy Kane, MC
Shan, Ghetto Boys, Too Short, and Sugar Hill Gang.
Reggie played a song Angel was not familiar
with.
When she heard…

I'm so tired of being alone
I'm so tired off on my own
Won't you help me girl…

"What is that?" Angel frowned as she requested
an answer of the old school music he was playing.
"Oh that's something you don't know about!"
Reggie snickered being glad that he had one up on her.
"That's something I don't need to know," Angel
shot back.
"Yo momma don't play no Al Green?"
"No. Not since my dad left she doesn't even
listen to music. My dad used to be into music. He
loves some Teddy Pendergrass." Angel smiled thinking
how she used to imitate Teddy singing *Turn Off The
Lights*.
"Where yo daddy at now? Is he dead?"
"He might as well be…" Angel thought about how
she called her father and found out the number was
disconnected. "…but he's around."
"Where he at?" Reggie feeling his question went
unanswered.
Angel went on to tell him how Luther taught her
to ride a bike, throw horseshoes, and play gin rummy.
When she thought she was Cinderella, her father was
the only one that put her up on the pedestal believing
she was Cinderella as much as Angel thought she was.
She talked about how he would say little crazy
sayings like "Empty wagons make the most noise" and
"If it looks like duck and quack like a duck, it's
gotta be a duck." She laughed telling him how her

father called her mother Tenda Brenda and she was his messiah. Reggie could tell from the conversation that Angel truly missed her father.

When everyone made it home, Angel didn't realize she had been on the phone with Reggie for at least four hours. Brooklin came barging into her room showing her a black and white polka dot dress and some black patent leather shoes that she was going to wear to graduation.

"Who you on the phone with?" Brooklin asked.

"Reggie."

"Tell Double R I said what's up and ask him where is Cordell?"

Reggie had heard her already and, before Angel could ask, he chattered, "Tell her he ain't in my pocket."

Angel looked at Brooklin. "He don't know."

"That ain't what I said!" Reggie yelled and Angel held the phone tightly to her ear.

"But that's what you meant," Angel chuckled.

"Yeah. Okay. So now you a mind reader," Reggie smirked.

"No. If I did, I would already know why people call you Double R." Angel's statement sounded like a threat.

"All you had to do was ask. I would have told you," Reggie shot back.

"Why do people call you Double R then?" Angel inquired.

"When I was little, I used to stutter. I would say things at least twice before it came out. So my friends just called me that."

"Why don't you stutter now?" Angel waited on his response.

"My parents got me some proper ass services. I went to speech therapy at school and they took me to the doctor."

"Your parents?"

"Yeah my parents. Why you ask me like that? I don't supposed to have parents? My mommy and my daddy look out for me," he said proudly.

"I asked because majority of everybody I know live with just their momma." Angel put emphasis on "momma" thinking Reggie sounded like a little baby.

"Well, now you know somebody who has both of their parents. My daddy gets up and goes to work every day. My mother used to work but she out on workers comp due to the fact she hurt her back on the job. She's a paramedic. She been off for the last two years. Her doctor hasn't released her to go back neither."

"She must have had some serious back injuries. My dad has a slipped disc in his back. For the record, I'm not saying that only single women are raising children. I know people have two parent homes."

"Oh what you saying is that I don't look like both of my parents live with me. That's so stereotypical!" Reggie shook his head.

"What does your father do?"

"He's an architect. He designs shit."

"Do you have any brothers and sisters?"

"I have one brother name Richard. He's older than me. I call him Richie-Rich. He always got his head in the books. He wants to be an Obstetrician and a Gynecologist."

"What's that?" Angel asked.

Reggie shook his head thinking Angel didn't know anything. "That's a doctor who has female patients."

"He sounds like my brother. My brother wants to become an entertainment slash corporate lawyer." Angel thought she said something to top what Reggie had just said.

"That's what's up!" Reggie was glad that they

at least had a few things in common.

"You think he look like Jam Master Jay?" Brooklin asked Angel as she sat down on Angel's full sized bed.

"We were just talking about that. I think he looks just like him." Angel said, looking up at Brooklin as she lay across the bed and then switching the conversation back to Reggie. "My sister thinks you look like Jam Master Jay, too."

Harlem walked into the room sporting his black and white pinstripe suit and black Stacy Adams. "How ya like me now!"

Angel and Brooklin laughed.

Brooklin looked at Harlem. "You gonna be the cleanest and finest light-skinned dude at graduation!"

Angel asked Reggie could she get his number so she could call him tomorrow. Realizing her siblings were in her room, it was time to wrap up their conversation. He thought she'd never ask as he recited his number with pride.

Brooklin left the beauty shop. She went to Blue Silk and Kelly had cut her hair in an asymmetrical style. The longest time was spent on straightening out her hair. Kelly had to press it because a relaxer had an opposite effect on Brooklin's hair. Instead of straightening it, it curled up. Angel had that same problem. Hair didn't matter to her. She kept her hair in a ponytail anyway.

When Brooklin made it up on the porch, C-Note pulled off in his green Jeep Cherokee. Before she made it in the door, Vincent walked up from out of nowhere. "Hey, Brooklin."

She jumped as she looked and saw this chocolate

figure. When her eyes met the gloomy eyes of Vincent, she spoke. "I'm glad that was you. Boy you scared the shit out of me!" Brooklin placed her right hand on her chest. She walked over to hug him. He was looking at her in a creepy way. It was similar to the way Pac did to Omar Epps in the movie *Juice* in the scene when he popped up at his locker. "I see you getting money now," Brooklin smiled.

"Oh that's why you kicked me to the curb? 'Cause I didn't have no money," Vincent said real slick.

"Naw boy. Why would you say something like that?" Her reason for leaving him was she only felt it was time to do someone different. C-Note became an asset because of the little stacks he was holding.

"You riding around with this nigga with his gold factory rims, Wagoner wood green Jeep Cherokee, and Kenwood pull-out." Vincent chattered like a stinking drunk man.

"Who Cordell? He just got that truck. He didn't have that when I met him."

"So what happened to us?" Vincent asked changing his tone and not cracking a smile.

"Vincent, nothing happened to us. I'm too young to be stuck with just one person. I'm just trying to have fun. You will always be my friend. Is that okay?" Brooklin waited on an answer.

"Naw! Hell naw! That's not okay, but I'm gonna make you love me! You can best believe that!" Vincent spoke with confidence as he walked away. His gloomy eyes perked up as he got louder each time he added a word on to his sentence.

Brooklin watched as he walked off. He disappeared just as fast as he appeared.

Brooklin went into the house and found Harlem playing Pac-Man on the Atari game system. "I'm surprised that thing still works."

Harlem didn't look up. "If you know how to take care of things correctly, you will never have to worry about it going out, giving up, or breaking down on you."

Everyone was getting in the car and heading to the graduation. Angel was wishing that Luther was there when somebody answered the number that he had given her. She had been calling that number hoping it would work. When she hung up, she whispered softly, "Daddy, you made a big mistake but someday we will be back together."

After the graduation, they went to Shoney's on South Grand Avenue to have lunch. When they entered, Vincent sat talking with Earl. He cut off his conversation with Earl as he jumped up from the booth and ran off to his car. When he returned, he walked up to Brooklin with his gift in his hand. Brooklin was startled as she stood at the food bar. "Vincent, are you following me?"

Vincent arched his eyebrows. "Girl naw. Earl and I were here already." He nodded towards Earl and she saw him sitting in the booth eating.

Brenda looked at Vincent. "I hope you got a gift for everybody."

Vincent kissed Brooklin on the cheek and walked away. Brooklin smiled as she wondered what was in the small neatly wrapped box. As soon as she made it to the table, she opened up the box. Tearing the wrapping off the box, she looked down to see the words Gucci imprinted on the brown box. When she opened the box, she saw a small bangle-like gold watch. Next to the watch were four interchangeable faces. She could wear an all gold watch or switch it up with trimmings of red, green, black, and fuchsia.

Harlem looked over to his mother and watched as she smiled. He shook his head in disgust. He wanted to tell Brooklin that she needed to give it back, but since his mother didn't disapprove, he thought his opinion was useless.

Chapter 6

THE BOYZ IN THE HOOD ARE ALWAYS HARD

"Let me see that screwdriver. These door handles on this cabinet is aluminum." Luther reached for the screwdriver from his toothless friend. That was the last piece of aluminum that they had grabbed from the condemned building. They had literally raped the house of every piece of scrap metal.

This was one of the many ways he got money to take care of his habit. He collected cans, pumped gas, cut grass, and washed cars. He never robbed and killed. He sort of kind of earned his keep. Except for when it went into abandoned buildings. He even sometimes sold fake dope to other junkies. He would get him some Ivory soap, bag it up in plastic and made it look just like crack.

Motha fuckas would be mad when their dope would just melt on their crack pipes. He had burned up so many dope sets on the south and west side that he had to purchase his dope on the north side of St. Louis.

After he got his dividends from the scraps, he headed to College and Carter. He was fiending so bad he didn't even notice Brooklin as he walked up to Flintstone.

"Let me get a fifty," Luther stated.

"Yo motha fucking money betta be right this

time," Flintstone shot back.

"Why you always gotta give me a hard time, hustling me and shit," Luther cried.

Brooklin sat there looking at her father as hatred filled her eyes. That was her first time seeing him out there buying dope, but it wouldn't be the last. Every time she saw her father, it appeared that everybody would give him a hard time. She wondered if she told them that that was her father would they let him get his crack and leave. She just kept it to herself. She was already embarrassed. So to save on some more embarrassment, she would hide or turn her back so he would never see her, but he did.

"Cuz it's my turn!" Scary yelled at Scooley as he walked up the next customer.

"Dude, this my set. You get yo turn when I get through!" Scooley retorted.

"It's like that?" Scary smirked.

"Yeah, cuz it's like that," Scooley shot back.

"You peep this shit?" Scary said to Peep Dog, knowing he was paying attention. That's how he earned his name. Because he was on point at all times. He peeped out everything.

Cuz, that's on my momma. Ain't nobody serving shit until I get done." Scooley kept chit chatting.

"On yo momma." Scary nodded.

"What, you hard of hearing?! Nigga on my momma. This N-hood. CNC cuz you don't wanna see it!" Scooley grabbed the brim of his Detroit Tigers fitted cap.

"Well, cuz, on the Bud ain't nobody finna sell shit on this dookie ass set!" Scary walked off and Peep Dog followed.

"Let me take you home before these niggas get to tripping out here." C-Note said to Brooklin. Brooklin followed him to the truck.

That would be the day that Scooley would have

wished he handled things a tad bit different. He didn't realize that Scary had disrespected him by saying dookie. Dookie is term used to disrespect "62 Deuce Crips." To disrespect the "Rolling Sixties," the term would be sissy. That's just like saying to someone "yo momma." The name calling was just that serious. In the gang world, to call a Crip a crab or call a blood a slob was showing the lack of respect for the person being called a crab or a slob.

Scooley simply ignored the statement. They had always claimed "Six Deuce," but when he put it on his momma, things changed. The Bud was no longer the just the Bud. They became the "Rolling Sixties" from the forty-four hundred block of the Bud. They distinguished themselves by wearing royal blue Seattle Mariners and Milwaukee Brewers fitted caps. They later wore Los Angeles Dodgers when others decided they didn't want to claim sixties, but choose "19 Long Beach." LBC is the set that Snoop Dogg previously claimed.

"Scooley fronted you out like that?" No Brains asked.

"Cuz, on my momma. He was like 'on my momma ain't nobody serving nobody until I get rid of all of my shit.' Like I told his ass, ain't nobody serving shit on that set," Scary told No Brains.

Cent Dog chimed in, "Well, let me go down there and let them dope fiends know we setting up shop up here on the Bud baby." He had been feeling out of place going over to their set to sell their dope. Now they could make moves on their own territory.

Chapter 7

CARS RIDE BY

"Is Reggie here?" Angel asked after she knocked on the front door and answered to the person on the other side of the door asking who it was.

No one answered. After a couple of minutes, Reggie appeared at the door. "You can come in."

Angel stood there for a moment. Not being sure if she wanted to cross that threshold, he stood there waiting. She eventually walked in. He led her through the living room, the dining room and straight into his room. She sat down at the desk as Reggie opted for the bottom bed on the bunk bed. He was listening to Ice Cube's *Amerikkka's Most Wanted*.

"Where's your television?" Angel asked looking around his bare room.

"We have to watch television together. We only have one TV. It's in the family room." Reggie answered not having a problem with not having a television in his room.

"You like cars?" Angel asked noticing his Hot Wheels collection. He had a car collection similar to the one Tyrese had in the movie "Baby Boy."

"I love cars!" Reggie squealed proudly.

They talked about their likes and dislikes which seemed for hours.

"Reggie, you and your friend can come and eat," Richard Sr. said firmly.

Angel felt out of place. She hadn't sat down at a dinner table since her father had left. She came out and entered the dining room. Reggie introduced her to his mother, father, and brother. They sat down to a dinner which was the beginning of more to come. After dinner, Reggie's father dropped her off at home. Reggie called Angel when he made it back home. They talked on the phone until the wee hours in the morning.

"What happened to your Cadillac?" Brooklin asked Vincent as he got out of a white four door Geo Prism.

"Ain't nothing happened to it. I can't drive two cars," Vincent grinned. "I bought this for you." Vincent dangled the keys in the air.

"Why you buy me a car and I can't drive?" Brooklin smiled.

"I bought you a Gucci watch so that you can know what time it is for us. So now I got you a car and I'm going to teach you how to drive." Vincent directed her to get in the car.

Brooklin learned how to drive within two hours. She had been so caught up with Vincent, she totally forgot about C-Note. He had been going through his own little dilemmas that he didn't give it a thought that maybe Brooklin was seeing someone else. Scary had acted upon his promise. One night as they approached College and Carter, the guys from Red Bud, which now went by 44 Bud, came from out of gangways as they unloaded their artillery. No one got hurt. Everybody was able to escape from the gunfire. They were just sending a message. Every night, they came through blasting. The dope fiends were scared to come through so they had no other choice but to go up on the Bud and get their dope. Some choose to go into other parts of the city, but the Bud was in walking distance for those that didn't have a car or enough gas to get to somewhere else.

Reggie's brother, Richard, had gotten himself a part-time job at the National grocery store up on Natural Bridge. He had been working for three months. He was trying to save his money up for his senior year of high school. He got off of work early and his father was not outside to get him so he decided to walk.

While he was on his way home, five masked men went into the National Supermarket to rob it. One person was going to each cash register and the other man was making the manager take him to the safe. The other three stood watch. At each entrance, some more masked individuals were on standby at each entrance. They were making sure that no one entered. Someone made a move and two of the masked men who were on lookout inside the store went berserk. They shot six workers and eight customers. Three were brutally murdered, the others suffered minor injuries.

As soon as Reggie stepped foot on the Bud, shots rang out.

BLOC BLOC BLOC!!
BOOM BOOM BOOM!!
SPAT SPAT SPAT!!
POCK POCK POCK!!

Richard died instantly, missing the massacre at his job and walking right into one as he reached his home.

Everyone was shooting from Stretch, Face, Scooley, B.K., Trippa, Ducky, Sweet Pea, C-Note, and T-Bone. They were just coming to retaliate with gun fire. They didn't set out to lay anybody down.

Before Richard was in the ground, his death was

avenged. Double R wasn't claiming anything and
neither was Richard. He wasn't hanging with his
friends and doing what they were doing. The death of
his brother led him down that path. No one would be
able to say who killed Richard until the autopsy
stated the type of gun that took his life. When he
heard about the beef, Reggie didn't care about the
type of gun. He felt that everyone from College and
Carter was responsible.

The day before Richard's funeral, Reggie
caught his first body. He and Scary were headed to
take care of some business. Reggie looked up and saw
Ducky coming out of the liquor store. Reggie walked
right up to him, put his Magnum up to Ducky's head.
Before he could run, one shot rang out and Ducky's
lifeless body fell to the ground.

Taking that life was nothing to it. Seeing him
lying there placed a pre-ejaculation substance in
Reggie's underwear. Nothing took over his body.
There was no rage or no fear. He had the natural born
killer instinct. From that day forward, he vowed
never to do drive-by. He wanted to make sure he always
hit his mark. If he was never to get right up on him,
there would always be the next time. His victims
would never get away from him. Dealing with him would
be the day they met their maker in his eye sight.

Angel attended Richard's funeral. Harlem,
Brooklin, and her mother attended the funeral with
her. Her late night phone calls with Reggie were
brought to a minimum. Anytime she wanted to talk to
Reggie, she would now have to page him. He had even
started hitting her off with a few dollars. She had
sensed his change but she chalked it up as him
mourning the loss of his brother.

Brooklin pulled up on the set looking for

C-Note. No one had seen him so she left. When she made it home, she realized that she hadn't picked Angel up from Reggie's house. She drove off before she even parked. Had C-Note came two seconds earlier, he would have seen her as she pulled off. Just as he got out of the car and was about to go up on the porch, he realized someone was shooting at him. He fell to the ground and prayed for dear life. He had just made it back from Black Pearl getting a tear drop tattooed under his right eye. Brenda came to the door five minutes after the gun shots had finished. She felt that was strange; she had never heard gunshots in her neighborhood except for New Year's. She became startled as she saw him lying on the ground. "Son, are you okay!" she screamed from her porch not knowing who she was talking to.

He stood up. "Mrs. Johnson, I am okay. As soon as I got out my car, somebody just started shooting."

"Well, Brooklin isn't here. She went to pick up Angel from over Reggie's house." Brenda told him unaware of the static that was taking place.

"Okay! Tell her I came by." C-Note quickly got into his car. He was now trying to figure out who was shooting at him. He realized that since Reggie and Angel were an item, he needed to stay away from Brooklin's house before he got hemmed up over there. That day, he vowed if Brooklin wanted to see him, she would have to come down his way. He didn't want anyone from his hood with a tear drop tattooed under their right eye in recognition of his death.

Brooklin watched Angel has she approached the car. It was something different about her. Being that her always smooth ponytail was messy added to the stupid grin she was wearing.

"You had sex with him?" Brooklin asked with

shocked and unsure tone in her voice.

"Yes, Brooklin, you ain't never had sex?" Angel was waiting on Brooklin to answer her.

"No. Daddy used to tell me that if I keep this tight, I would be considered special. Let the boy get sex from somebody else 'cause that's all they want is some pussy anyway. Just like you believe in God, you better start believing in me." Brooklin cried out.

"Stop! Brooklin stop the car! NOW!" Angel screamed.

Brooklin pulled over and Angel hopped out of the car. Brooklin thought that if Angel didn't want to hear about if she believed in God, she might as well believe in her speech. The tears flooding her eyes with the sight of her father made her pull over.

"Daddy, Daddy!" Angel ran up behind Luther. He turned around and smiled. She hugged him and was happy she didn't smell that stench. "Daddy, where you headed to? You wanna go with us and get something to eat?"

He smiled at his beautiful daughter. He took his hand off his pistol. He nodded yes as he led Angel back to the car. He knew his messiah had come because he was about to do the inevitable to the kid who always disrespected him when he came to get his crack. C-Note had escaped death twice that night.

"Where we supposed to take him?" Brooklin asked. The hate could be felt as she spoke.

"'Him' is your father and he's going home with us so he can get a hot bath and something to eat. So drive this car," Angel instructed.

"What momma gone say?" Brooklin asked as she pulled off.

"We will cross that bridge when we get to it," Angel said.

Luther smiled to himself with pride. That's what he always said to his Tenda Brenda.

They pulled up in front of the house. He smiled as he looked at the house with the beautiful landscaping. Speaking with admiration, Luther said, "This sure is a big house."

"Wait until you see the inside," Angel said as they walked up on the porch.

The walk to the front door was quiet. Then Brooklin's car chirped. They all turned around and looked at the car. Brooklin and Angel appeared to be taken by surprise.

Luther noticed their looks of confusion and had to ask, "You have an alarm on that car that you don't know about?"

"Not that I know of," Brooklin answered with a state of confusion.

Luther walked in and Harlem's eyes lit up like a little child on Christmas morning. He got up and reached for his father's hand, pulled him towards him, and embraced him tightly. Luther just smiled. He was wishing Brooklin would open up to him like Harlem and Angel did.

Brenda looked stunned. "Hey Luther! Where they find you?"

"Out and about. Angel trying to bathe and feed me, if you don't mind," Luther stated.

Before Brenda could answer, Harlem intervened. "Daddy, I think I got some gear you can fit."

~ 53 ~

"I'm quite sure you do. He looks like he only weigh a buck fifty soaking wet. Those damn clothes gonna swallow his ass!" Brooklin blurted out before she walked off, "Lord, help them all!"

No one commented. Brenda was on her way to meet her estranged lover but she called and cancelled. The day she longed for had arrived. Luther stayed around for two weeks. He didn't even bother to step out the door. They laughed for hours talking about old times.

Angel invited Reggie over to meet her father. They played cards and a few rounds of dominoes. That was the happiest Brenda had been since Luther had left years ago.

Harlem was coming in the house when he saw his mother's lover slowly ride by. He waved at Harlem and Harlem waved back. He went into the house and was taken aback when he saw Reggie sitting there having a conversation with Luther as if they had known each other for years.
While Luther was left at the house alone, he went through some old photographs. He smiled as he reminisced about the past. As he continued, he noticed his presence was disappearing from the pictures. He looked around the room and noticed what all Brenda had accomplished without him. He realized he hadn't contributed to none of that. Luther was feeling as though he had failed as a husband and father. He left in search of the one thing that didn't judge him and didn't care about anything he hadn't accomplished. He left and didn't look back.

When Luther made it to his place of residence, he bitched and complained on how she was worried about him. She thought he was dead. He just looked at Maxine. He knew she wasn't concerned about him and his whereabouts. She just didn't have anybody to go get her crack. She was what you considered undercover. She got up and went to work every day. She worked at an area clinic as a nurse. She met Luther one day when he came in to donate some blood during a blood drive the clinic was having.

Maxine felt he was a nice looking man and was worth cleaning up. She had three kids herself: two girls and one boy. Luther sat wondering everyday about how he was there helping someone else raise their kids and couldn't be there for his own. It wasn't as though he was providing for them financially. He was helping with homework, cooking dinner, and doing odds and ends around the house. What kept him there was the fact that Maxine liked what he liked.

"Where? Over on Glasgow?" Reggie asked.

"That's a damn Blood set! They call it Beam Street. Those cats be all beamed up with red and big ass guns." Peep Dog added his two cents.

"Fuck dem slob ass niggas!" Scary waved his hand and put up the middle finger.

"Those dudes over there getting money. Some dude named LA Ray got them booming. From what I hear, that nigga Rance run it around there." Midnight supplied his bit of info from what he heard through the street vine.
Reggie turned to Midnight. "That nigga with that tricked out Cutlass?"
Reggie and Peep Dog got in the base head car

Reggie had rented. Scary and Midnight got in the car Scary had rented. They were following each other to the gas station.

Peep Dog turned his head, "Look! There go that nigga Rance right there!"

Reggie pulled onto the Amoco gas station lot towards the exit that Rance was bound to take to leave the gas station. Right when he was about to pull off, Reggie was right behind him. He had just sat there waiting on him. Scary bumped Rance's bright red Cutlass so hard they tapped Reggie's car.

Rance slowly got out of the car wearing an all red sweatshirt and blue jeans. He pulled his red St. Louis Cardinals fitted cap slowly over his eyes. His deep chocolate skin went unnoticed but the whites of his eyes gleamed. Rance made it to the back of his car to glance at the fender bender. All he heard was Midnight saying, "I got forty-four ways…"

Midnight hadn't finished his statement before Rance knew he was being carjacked. He knew he should have gassed up before he met with LA Ray. Now whoever was behind this caper just made a quick come up of the five bricks of cocaine he had in the trunk alone. Rance had to be kin to Carl Lewis due to the mad dash he made to get away. Midnight hopped in Rance's car and they all skirted off.

Rance's face was posted on all the local news stations. He was killed execution style on Glasgow the same day he was carjacked. The motive and shooter went unknown. His car was found near the junkyard on Hall Street raped of everything from the tires to the seats in the car.

Chapter 8

TELL YO DADDY TO PAGE ME!

Angel lay across her bed. This was the third time this week that she had paged Reggie and he hadn't called right back. He had been doing this for the last month or two.

She began to play in his pager. She would put 304 because upside down it looked like "hoe" or she would put 187 because that's the penal code for murder. She then went from 304 and 187 to just counting in his pager. After the beep, she just put one and pressed the pound sign. Before she realized, she had made it to one hundred. She was furious. She felt she was giving up her goods and he should come running to her beck and call.

She began to cry realizing she was about to be stood up when she looked at the clock and it read 11:47 p.m. Reggie was taking her to see Boyz in the Hood. She was becoming disappointed in men and understood why Brooklin hated Luther so much up until the phone rang.

"Hello!"

"Angel, I'm sorry but Scary got killed tonight," Reggie cried.

"What happened?" Angel began to become sadden by the bad news. Reggie and Scary had gotten so close since Richard had gotten murdered.

"He was picking up Monica because she was going to the show with us. They was driving by and seen him getting out the car. Monica said they yelled 'on my momma it's like that' and start shooting," Reggie whimpered. "If he had picked me up first, that wouldn't have happened and Monica's pregnant."

"Pregnant? She's only fourteen. She's a year older than me. Now she has to raise that baby alone and she's just a baby herself."

"No she don't. I'm going lookout for her." Reggie shook his head.

"She seen who did that to him?" Angel didn't want to appear selfish but she was glad that Reggie wasn't there. She grasped the fact that could have been there in Monica's shoes.

"Yeah, it was those niggas Brownie and Scooley. It's killa for those cats on sight. Anyway, you think you can get out the house?"

"I have to see if Harlem's sleep because my momma is not here."

"Call me and put eleven twenty-two, if it's cool to come through. And quit playing on my pager. I will call you back as soon as I can."

"Alright." Angel hung up the phone.

Reggie was on his way when he looked in his pager and saw 1122. He was already sitting outside her house. Vincent walked up to his car.

"This how you rolling?" Vincent reached in and shook Reggie's hand as he sat in the beat up blue Oldsmobile.

"Naw. This a clucker car." Reggie got out.

This was nothing out of the norm. Vincent always shot the breeze with Reggie when he came through to see Angel.

"My homey got knocked today." Reggie shook his head holding back his tears.

"Sorry to hear that," Vincent replied.

"Shit is crazy and things are getting out of hand. I don't even wanna go home 'cause I think them niggas laying down in my gangway waiting on me."

"You know who it is?" Vincent showed his concern.

"You know ole boy Brooklin be fucking with, C-Note?"

"Yeah!" Vincent was all ears.

"His lil' crew caught my boy sleeping. He was picking up his chick. We were supposed to be on our way to the show."

Brooklin pulled up as they stood there and talked. At the same time, Angel walked out the door. Vincent said his good-byes. Angel and Brooklin talked with Reggie before Brooklin walked into the house.

Reggie pulled off before Brooklin made it in the house. She stopped as she heard her car chirp. She thought she was tripping because her car would chirp every time she was about to open her door. She ignored it thinking that maybe that was someone else's car.

"Your sister is sleeping with the enemy," Reggie looked over at Angel.

"Any who." Angel didn't really want to talk about it. She paused and then spoke, "How you know C-Note doesn't feel the same way?" Angel looked back at Reggie.

"Fuck C-Note! They may as well call him Casper again. It's about to be some slow singing for that dude. I hope his momma know six motha fuckers that can carry that ass 'cause I'm saving his ass for last. I'm doing them niggas one by one."

Angel was astonished listening to him talk. She looked over and saw a totally different person from the boy she saw sitting down having dinner with his parents.

They made it to the Vegas Inn. They pulled up and Reggie got out of the car. He came back with keys in his hand. The Vegas Inn was a little raunchy hotel in the hood. Being that Reggie was only fifteen, he couldn't get a room anywhere else. He may not have feared going home, but he couldn't. He knew evil awaited him and his father made it clear to him.

"I'm not about to lose you to the streets, too!" Richard Sr. yelled as he threw and broke Reggie's pager.

"Cuz! You fucking with my money!" Reggie flinched at his father.

As Richard Sr. was about to tear into Reggie, he paused. He was looking at the barrel of a semi-automatic weapon.

"Only one man can live here!" He turned and walked away with tears in his eyes. He realized he had already lost his son.

"What kind of gun is that?" Angel asked as Reggie laid it down on the nightstand next to the bed. She looked at the big black handgun with holes around the barrel.

Reggie picked it back up. "This here is called a Tech-Nine. I got this from Nine. This all he carries."

Angel felt a sense of safety. The thought of being scared never crossed her mind. They stayed at the raunchy motel for the night and Reggie dropped Angel off at home in the morning.

"This the homeboy Vincent. He getting that real

money with Earl and K-Rock." Reggie introduced Vincent to his crew. "He fucks with Angel's sister Brooklin."

Lay-Loc looked him over. He knew Brooklin fucked with C-Note and he instantly felt that Vincent had a motive and purpose to be gracing them with his presence. "We 'bout to ride down on them niggas C-Note and 'em. You rolling?"

Vincent looked at Reggie. "Naw. That's y'all beef. I came over here to discuss some money business."

Cent Dog nodded. "Money! My type of conversation. Show a nigga how to make a dollar outta fifteen cent."

Vincent ran the plan down and told them to meet them in two hours.

Vincent looked at his watch before looked over at Earl. "Where these little niggas at?"

"Yeah, that's what I'm saying. I knew those lil' niggas ain't trying to get no real money. I have my ear to the streets. They just too busy trying to kill one another over some senseless ass bullshit." K-Rock was ready to go. Sitting on the Bud with the war taking place, he didn't want to become a casualty.

"Get on the motha fucking flo'! I ain't afraid to use this!" Tyrone looked at the barrel of the Tech-Nine wishing he could snatch off the black ski-mask.

No one said a word. Lay-Loc was tearing up the floor with his crowbar. Reggie, No Brains, Clack, and D.A. held Earl's brother at gunpoint.

"Bingo!" Lay-Loc popped the last weak plank in

the floor after he scooted the bed over. "These niggas got twelve bricks up under here!"

Lay-Loc grabbed the bricks of cocaine. He jumped when he heard the first gunshot.

No Brains did all of Earl's brothers in. That wasn't part of the plan. He just didn't want to be worried about some more people trying to take his head off.

Right as Vincent was about to pull off, they pulled up in a blue mini-van. Earl didn't see him, but K-Rock did. Vincent saw them as soon as they pulled onto the street as he sat in the back seat of the white Cadillac.

Reggie walked up on the right side and Midnight appeared out of the shadows. He had been standing in the gangway watching them with his infrared beam. Had Vincent pulled off, Midnight was pulling the trigger.

"So what y'all trying to spend?" Earl said as he walked around to Reggie.

"Nineteen." Reggie looked him straight in his eyes.

"I only let them thangs go for twenty-one." Earl waited on his response.

Reggie pulled his Milwaukee Brewers fitted cap down over his eyes. Trying to slow his breathing down to the rhythm of his normal heartbeat," he replied. "I'll let Vincent know something tomorrow."

"Alright. Get at 'em then." Earl dapped his fist and got back in the car.

When Vincent pulled up, there was nothing but police cars, evidence trucks, ambulances and yellow tape. They sat and watched the scene from afar. No one wanted to walk up and catch a case considering everything that was in the house.

As the black body bags left the porch of the dope house that Earl and his brothers worked from, he passed out. K-Rock cried. Vincent couldn't believe what was happening. He didn't care about what had happened to Quincy, Ulysses, Paul and Tyrone. He sat there thinking that they should have been spared. He was amongst those ones that should have been taken out.

Reggie and his crew were ready to put in some more work. They jumped into the van and peeled out. When they approached C-Note and his crew, they cut the lights off. Reggie was driving. As soon as he spotted Brooklin, he cut the headlights on. Peep Dog saw her too.

"There go Brooklin!" Peep spoke out softly.

They drove on down the street slowly. Reggie looked at her thinking to himself she needed to be thanking the man upstairs for that one. She was about to become a casualty. He thought of how she was always talking nonsense about how people better believe in her.

Lay-Loc locked eyes with C-Note and pointed his fingers at him as if he fired a gun. C-Note watched as they drove off. He knew exactly why his life was spared. He wanted to turn to Brooklin and tell her that he now believed in her just as well as he believed in the Lord. He thought she was crazy for saying shit like that, but this day his thoughts were different.

C-Note held Angel tightly. He watched as a white short dog Cadillac rode past them with three passengers. Vincent never looked their way, but Earl did. Vincent knew Brooklin from anywhere, even in the dark. He thought someone of his status needed an arm piece like Brooklin by his side. Eye candy like her was only for the supreme individuals.

"Ain't that Brooklin?" K-Rock asked. He knew the answer before his question was answered.

K-Rock looked at Vincent. "Don't tell me my boys lost their lives over your bitch!"

That's exactly what Vincent wanted them to think. His whole plan had backfired. When they got back to the spot, somebody was supposed to be alive and be able to tell the story. He was going to start some static with the guy that was fucking with Brooklin and use the Mac boys as his enforcers. The boys would retaliate against them. He had his reasons for not wanting to ask Reggie and his crew to put in some work for him. Now he was left with two of the softest niggas in the Lou. Together, they weren't about to throw rice at a wedding.

Chapter 9

NOBODY MOVES NOBODY GETS HURT

Richard Sr. sat up in his bed. He looked over at his wife and found her fast asleep. The sound of breaking glass awakened him. He continued to sit and listen. He had repaired the window six times. Every time he went down to the basement, nothing had been removed. There was no trace that anyone had entered, but there was just evidence of a broken window. He got up and walked to the kitchen. Looking out of the window, he saw Reggie running out of the yard.

Confusion crossed his mind as he wondered why Reggie would be breaking into the house. Reggie had taken up residency with Richard Sr.'s younger brother, Robert. Reggie's uncle worked nights at the post office and slept during the day. Richard Sr. decided to put a piece of removable Plexiglas up to the window. He didn't know why Reggie was sneaking in and out, and he didn't feel the need to stop him. Although he wanted him out of the house, he knew he was okay every time he popped up. Richard Sr. soon realized why he was coming in the house. He kept the secret amongst them.

Each set had increased. People started associating with either CNC or the Bud. Each set was getting their props. The work they were putting in was getting recognized throughout the Lou. The drama was spreading like wildfire. People wanted to be affiliated with the set that was known to go all out.

Reggie had met up with his crew. They were spray painting a vacant building that could be seen by all passersby. In blue spray paint, No Brains put up "R.I.P. Richie" and "R.I.P. Scary." Gang graffiti was scattered all over the building. Caliber wrote "62K." Midnight began to write R.I.P.'s for C-Note, Stretch, Playa, Flintstone, Sweet Pea, B. K., Scooley, Trippa, Slick, and Face. Cent-Dog came right behind him and crossed all of those names out.

"You been down Carter?" Scooley asked C-Note.
"Nope! Why?" C-Note answered.
"Those niggas dun hit the wall up with six deuce killa and crossed out all our names. You know what that mean?" Scooley was amped.
"What it mean?" C-Note didn't expect him to answer because he knew what it meant.
"They gon' kill us!" Scooley cried in a joking type of manner.
C-Note led Scooley to his truck. They took a ride because C-Note wanted to see the graffiti for himself. They pulled up on Carter. They just sat and looked at the wall and at the activity taking place down the street. Nine was sitting back in the cut taking it all in. Peep Dog saw the truck. "Aye, keep y'all heads up. Those niggas sitting on the corner!"
Clack, Caliber, and Midnight looked in their direction. They continued to serve their customers as Peep Dog and Nine observed the scene. Once they noticed they had been spotted, they skirted off.

"What year and how much is the grey SS?" Reggie asked the salesman as Midnight followed behind the both of them.

"This right here, my friend, is a 1986 and the asking price is eleven grand," the salesman stated.

"I'll give you eight right now for it," Reggie spoke with confidence.

"Well, my friend, I'd say you got you a deal!" the chubby salesman grinned.

They shook hands and did the necessary paper work. The salesman sat there and counted every last dime. Reggie looked down at his pager. He didn't recognize the number so he paid it no attention. Five minutes later, his pager went off again with the same number, but this time 911 was behind it. He asked to use the telephone. Monica was calling him to let him know that she had had the baby. "Her name is Keena Brown. I tried to keep it as close to Keith as I could. R, she looks just like Scary. He really marked my baby. I'm sitting up here black as night and this baby high yellow!" Monica chuckled.

"What hospital are you at?"

"Up here on Delmar at Regional."

"When I get through with this business, I am going to stop up there. Do you need anything?"

"I am hungry." Monica licked her lips.

"Alright. I am going to stop at Burger King. That's cool?"

"Yeah! Get me a Whopper, some fries, and an apple pie."

Reggie laughed. "I gotcha. Give me 'bout an hour and I'll swing through there."

"See you then." Monica hung up the phone.

"What you doing, Harlem?" Angel asked as she stood at his door.

"Filling out some college applications. I am

only going to apply to three. They are asking for $25 each for application fees so I am trying to narrow it down." Harlem looked up at Angel. "I really don't care where I go as long as I get away from here. What are you up to?"

"I was coming to see if you wanted to go skating with us. Brooklin and I are going to Saints out in Olivette."

"I'll pass. I'm not trying to be around y'all gang banging ass friends and a sister that thinks she can walk on water. You need to be careful before you get caught up and can't find your way out. What happened to the Cinderella fairytales? You far from Never Never Land!" Harlem spoke with sincerity. He wanted to go into depth but he figured why waste his breath. Harlem knew Angel was going to do what she felt what was best for Angel.

"Have a nice time." Harlem said nonchalantly.

"Ah Harlem!" Angel looked into her brother's room. "Apply to as many colleges you want." Angel threw him a bundle of money, shut his door and went on her way.

She paused in the mirror to see how she looked as she adjusted her side ponytail. She thought she was geared in her purple Nautica shirt and purple Guess jeans. Angel made it to the bottom of the steps.

"Angel, how I look?" Brooklin raised her arms.

"Used up!" Angel laughed referring to the Used denim jean outfit with orange tint. The laughing stopped when they heard the car alarm. Brooklin went over to the window. She was trying to figure out why she always heard that noise.

"I am going to get that checked out Monday morning."

"What?" Angel asked.

"My car. It chirps all the time. Every time I come in the house, it chirps." Brooklin began to sound spooked.

"There's nothing wrong with your car. Why don't you have Vincent get it checked out? Or maybe God is trying to tell you something!" Angel thought taunting her would make her think about the craziness she would put on about her beliefs. Angel didn't understand why her sister would compare herself to such a supreme being. It really confused her. She could remember the first time Brooklin asked the crazy question.

"Angel, do you believe in me?"

"Why would I believe in you?" Angel asked.

"Do you believe in God?" Brooklin waited on the answer.

"What kind of question is that? Of course I believe in God!"

"Then tell me this. Have you ever seen God?"

"Brooklin, I don't have to see Him to believe. I know He's there. He is the reason I have life. He is the reason that you and I are able to wake up every day. You been to church, you know the story."

"Angel, here it is you see me every day. I talk with you, walk with you, I cry with you, and I even share pain with you. So just like you believe in God you should believe in ME." Brooklin pointed to herself.

"Brooklin, I do believe in you," Brooklin smiled thinking she had convinced her sister of her insanity. "I believe you're crazy as hell conjuring up enough courage to say stupid stuff like that!"

Harlem counted the money. He didn't have to wonder where his little sister had gotten five hundred dollars from. He just wondered what she did to get it. Harlem headed to Angel's room in search of some answers. When he reached the door, he changed his mind. She was not there. He figured he'd just talk to her when she came back. He resumed doing what he was doing.

Midnight and Reggie entered the elevator in the hospital. When they reached the maternity ward and the doors opened there stood this girl that looked like Janet Jackson when she did the movie "Poetic Justice." She had the long thick braids and all.

"Baby girl, what's yo name?" Reggie asked in his Mack mode voice.

"Tawanna. Who wanna know?"

"Double R, baby girl."

Tawanna looked him over. She was impressed with his heavy starched sky blue Guess blue jeans, his crisp white thick-t, and his fresh pair of Air Jordan's. She took his number in a hurry.

Midnight placed the red roses and the balloons displaying "Congratulations" on the side of Monica's bed. Reggie handed her the bag of food. He let her know they couldn't stay long because they we going to Saints. She thanked them for coming and they went on their way.

Reggie pulled up on the Walgreens parking lot. Midnight sat in the car crushing the Tylenol threes. Reggie made it back to the car and he threw Midnight the bottle of Robitussin.

The music was loud and roller skates were click clacking. For Reggie and Midnight, things were moving sort of slow. They had sipped on some Syrup and were sliding on cloud nine.

Reggie walked past the trophy case. Before he knew what had happened, he was thrown into the case. A crowd began to gather around as C-Note began to dog walk Reggie. Midnight was no help. By the time he was about to react, Midnight was on the ground getting the shit kicked out of him. Security didn't make it over to him soon enough. Damage was done and C-Note and his crew dispersed through the crowd.

One of Angel's classmates informed her of what had just taken place. As she shifted through the crowds, she could hear people saying how one dude got stomped so bad he was throwing up blood. She saw Reggie sitting on the bench in the front of the skating rink. His shirt was bloody and his left eye was swollen shut. He resembled the elephant man. The sight brought tears to Angel's eyes. The paramedics arrived. Midnight was placed on the stretcher. They did him in. Reggie suffered minor injuries. The night at the skating rink ended early.

Angel and Reggie were watching an episode of "Martin." His uncle had just left for work. As the commercial played, Reggie spoke. "Do C-Note come over your house to see Brooklin?"

"He used to. He doesn't anymore. I don't think

she want him and Vincent bumping heads."

"You think she can get him to come over?" Reggie watched her reactions. This was her test. He needed to know just how much she was down for him.

"She probably could, but she not. You ain't bringing that shit to my house. You keep that shit in the streets." Angel couldn't believe he had asked her that! She sat quiet for the next twenty minutes. When "Martin" went off, she asked him to take her home.

As they were driving down Newstead Avenue, Reggie saw the green Jeep Cherokee. He surveyed the area. C-Note stood out in the open talking on a payphone. Reggie circled the block. He came back up the street so C-Note would be on his side of the car. Reggie pulled right up behind C-Note who was deep in the conversation he had taking place. Reggie put the car in park, sat on the edge of the car door and let loose. C-Note hit the ground. When he fell, Reggie pulled off.

"Cordell! Cordell!" Brooklin screamed through the phone. C-Note looked himself over and then stood to his feet. He told Brooklin he would call her when he made it home.

"Why the hell you do that bullshit with me in this got damn car!" Angel was furious. She looked up at the car and began talking out loud to herself. "This nigga gon have me locked up in somebody's jail. I can't believe this bullshit. You may as well told me to drive. Got me a part of some damn drive-by." She talked the whole way home. Reggie wasn't paying her any attention. He was trying to get to a phone to find out who had just paged him.

~ 72 ~

Angel got out of the car and slammed the door. "Next time ask me if I want to bring the noise with you."

Reggie made it back home. "Anybody paged a pager?"

"I did," the female voice said seductively.

"Who dis?"

"This Tawanna."

"Oh what's up with you?"

"I'm trying to see you."

"Straight!"

"Naw crooked," Tawanna smirked.

"Where you stay at? I'll come swoop you."

"You know where Anderson is?"

"From off Taylor."

"Yeah."

"What's the address?"

"You know that nigga just got through shooting at me!" C-Note said to Flintstone.

"What you expect? You beat his ass yesterday. He probably think he laid you down. You may need to lay low for a while."

Teresa Seals

"I can't make no money in the house," C-Note stated.

"I know this dude named Vincent that moves weight. We can get some work from him and sell out them other cats and let them stand out there on that hot ass set." Flintstone dragged on his piece of marijuana laced with crack cocaine.

"Cuz what is that smell?" C-Note frowned up.

"I mixed some crack-cocaine in with my weed." Flintstone continued to inhale.

"You can keep that shit. Holla at dude and get back with me. Peace! I'm out." C-Note gave Flintstone some dap and left him by his lonely.

"Reggie what you doing?" Angel asked.

"I ain't doing nothing but doing what I was doing before you caught your little attitude and wanted to go home," Reggie whispered.

"And what is that!" Angel screamed.

"Watching television."

"Reggie, say my name."

"For what?"

"I know you got somebody over there! So say my got damn name!"

"Oh, Angel!" Reggie cried out.

~ 74 ~

Tawanna smiled as Reggie held himself while his dick threw up white cream. Reggie had just lost his virginity in the head game department. She had deep throated the shit out of him. She thought she had got her next victim. Tawanna thought to herself it won't be long before he'd be tricking off his cash.

"What the fuck is you doing?" Angel was trying to make out the sounds.

Reggie hung up the phone. Angel started calling back to back and blowing his pager up. 187 came across the screen several times.

Chapter 10

Jang-a-Lang

C-Note was getting his money up as he was able to lay back and chill. He finally wanted to meet the connection that Flintstone only did business with. With a knock on the door, Vincent entered. They made the exchange and Vincent left. C-Note never tripped off the nigga that was bringing the dope to him. Instead, he thought he had it like that.

Harlem received several acceptance letters. He decided on going to Alabama A&M. He figured that would put enough distance between him and his family. He was hoping that Brooklin would have wanted to come along, but he knew she wasn't going to leave Angel behind.

Harlem and Brooklin prepared for graduation all week long. Dr. Dre's "The Chronic" played in the background as everyone got dressed. Angel had gotten in touch with Luther. He was sitting downstairs talking with Brenda as their children were getting ready.

When they came down the steps, Brenda had the Polaroid camera in hand. Flash! Pictures instantly came out of the camera. They posed together. Everyone switched up making sure everybody was a part of a picture before they headed to the graduation. Luther was so proud to be a part of this. He felt a little awkward around Reggie. Earlier that week, he saw Luther begging some dude to pump his gas.

They walked out to get in Brenda's car. Angel locked the door. She looked over in the neighbor's yard and saw a bunch of big black crows.

Reggie rolled through the hood with Tawanna sitting in his passenger seat. He was flossing his seventeen inch all chrome Radial 100 spoke Dayton's. He was waiting on Angel to page him when she left the graduation. He was meeting them at the Esquire on Clayton. They were going to check out the movie *Menace II Society*. When he got the page, Tawanna was getting dropped off.

"You ready to re-up?" Vincent spoke to C-Note on the phone.

"Yeah. You coming through?" C-Note asked.

"I'll be there in about ten minutes." Vincent hung up.

Reggie got the page. He saw 1122 come across his pager. He told Tawanna he'd get up with her later. She tried to bless him with her vicious head game, but he turned it down. When she caught an attitude, Reggie was instantly turned off. She got out of the car.

Reggie screamed, "How the fuck you gonna get mad at me 'cause I won't let you suck my dick?! Nasty Bitch!" He skirted off before she made it to the sidewalk.

"What you up to?" Vincent asked as he entered through C-Note's back door.

"Man my gal didn't even invite me to her graduation." Vincent could hear the hurt in C-Note's voice.

"Yo gal?" Vincent looked at him sideways.

"Dude it's a long story."

"I got time."

C-Note gave him the run down from beginning to end. Vincent was glad to find out that Brooklin hadn't given his goods up. He wanted to be her first. After a while, Vincent started thinking of other things as C-Note continued to talk. He was so hyped that he asked Vincent to take him to go get on those Bud Cats. Vincent agreed. C-Note put on his black t-shirt and his fitted San Diego baseball cap.

Vincent pulled right into the alley. He was directly behind the spot that Reggie and his boys stood out in front of. Vincent followed C-Note into the yard. Vincent caught his first body. Now he didn't have anything to worry about. Now Brooklin would be all his. So he thought anyway.

"I didn't like the way that movie ended. Cane should have lived," Brooklin said to Harlem.

"Well, that's simply the way it goes. Shit, that's just a movie. Niggas dying in my hood every day," Reggie spat.

"I don't care what nobody says. That movie was cold. That's going on my top ten. That dude O-Dog got down. That dude Chauncey was a straight bitch." Angel followed Reggie to his car.

Reggie's pager went off. He grabbed it from his side. He was trying to figure out who was paging him from Angel's house. "Somebody paging me from your house," he said strangely.

Angel and Reggie walked back towards the movie theatre. Harlem pulled alongside of them and rolled down the window. "Where y'all going?"

"Somebody paged me from yawls house," Reggie told Harlem.

Angel called home. Her mother asked her where was Brooklin. Angel let her know that they had just left out of the show. That's when Brenda burdened them with the bad news. Angel looked dazed as she hung up the phone.

"Baby what's wrong?" Reggie asked.
Brooklin was walking towards Angel. She had just got through exchanging numbers with a dude name Ray. He had pulled up on her in his brown Riviera. He was clean cut. Standing about five foot seven. Chocolate complexion with cornrows. His bedroom eyes were what got Brooklin's attention. She noticed the daze Angel was in and totally ignored the chocolate drop she had just met. She brought her conversation to an end and ran over to her sister.

"Angel what's wrong?!" Brooklin yelled.

"Somebody killed C-Note!" Angel yelled back.

Harlem looked at Reggie and together they both shared no emotion. Angel held Brooklin as she broke down crying.
Harlem drove Brooklin home. She cried the

entire way. Reggie followed behind. His Kenwood played smooth sounds like Troop's *All I Do Is Think of You* and Levert's *Baby I'm Ready*.

Luther walked up on the set to comp. Flintstone didn't even hassle him today. Luther wanted to know what was wrong with him because he didn't have to go through the changes to get his dope. When Flintstone told him, he asked him was Brooklin with him. He and Flintstone talked about his past and how Brooklin was disappointed with him. Flintstone took it all in. He had even given him something extra.

Brenda didn't allow Brooklin to go to his funeral. She didn't know what was going on. She took Brooklin to her house in Ladue. She didn't know if anyone would be after her daughter or what. She was trying to convince Angel to go. Harlem stepped in to persuade her. She was not going. Harlem was preparing himself to leave. He couldn't understand why his sisters were so caught up in the game that broke up their family. He wanted to be ashamed of them for indulging in the benefits of the drug dealing. Harlem had even gotten mad at himself for not giving that money back to his baby sister.

Reggie rode past his set. No one was outside but a few detectives and the crime scene unit. He pulled up behind his parent's house. When he got in the basement, his father startled him. He let him know what had happened across the street. His father gave him a hug and told him to be careful. He went upstairs and walked out the back door.

Vincent sat outside with Earl on his front porch. Earl reminisced about when they were kids. He laughed thinking about how everybody always hung out at Auntie's house. Earl had lost his brothers and K-Rock was sucking that glass dick. "From sugar to shit!" was how he summed it up. Vincent just sat there listening.

Vincent was the devil in sheep's clothing. He convinced C-Note to walk to the set of his enemies, saying he would help him put in some work. C-Note was shot at point blank range in his face. C-Note's mother was only able to identify him from his birthmark which was on his buttocks, on the left. When she saw the mark that represented a crescent moon, she just broke down and cried. His ceremony was closed casket. His face couldn't be reconstructed at all.

Chapter 11

KILLING ME SOFTLY

"May I speak to Ray?"

Ray blew into the cartridge before he placed the game into the Nintendo game system. "This Ray. Who dis?"

"Dis be Brooklin."

"I thought yo fine ass wasn't ever gon' call me."

He paused the game and lay back thinking of that chocolate bombshell he had met a while back.

"So what does Brooklin like to do to for fun?"

"You know I don't have any hobbies. My little sister loves rap music, she loves watching movies, and her favorite color is purple. I started off liking purple but any color is good for me."

"Well, I'm going to expose you to some things I like to do. Then you can tell me if you like them or not."

"Some things like what?" Brooklin asked.

"What are you doing tomorrow?" Ray retorted.

"Nothing."

"Call me in the morning."

They hung up and Ray continued to play his game.

Harlem was getting his last items together. The day came and he was finally leaving. He packed the U-Haul Reggie paid for and he headed on down the highway. He didn't even see Brooklin before he left. He left St. Louis not ever wanting to return. Every memory was being left in the Lou and his fresh start was in Alabama. He took the money Reggie had given him as a going away present with no hesitation. He knew he was being very hypocritical, but he used it to his benefit.

Harlem found it so difficult to relax around his family. He couldn't find the solitude he preferred. It bothered him that his mother was too involved with a married man. She was not paying attention to her girls, who he felt needed her most. His sisters were now too indulged in the lifestyle that was the cause of Luther's absences. It was tearing him apart that he didn't know how to go about talking some sense into them. When Luther walked out, he experienced his mother facing one little crisis after another. He wondered why it found its way into their home. He thought going away to school would deter him from growing weary of all the problems that surfaced. He feared that he wouldn't receive the support from Brenda, Brooklin, or Angel. He didn't panic or go out without a bang; he just ran away.

Morning approached and Brooklin hadn't slept

a wink. She anticipated on what the day brought. As soon as Brooklin got dressed, she called Ray. She was so ready to get out of the house. She had been cooped up in that apartment for two months.

Within a month, Ray had taken her horseback riding, go-cart riding, and snorkeling. She wasn't ready for the bungee jumping. When he introduced her to the game of chess, she became intrigued with all the different things he knew. In moments, they became inseparable.

On one particular night, Brooklin invited Ray in when they came back from having dinner with his sister and her children. She learned that his mother had recently passed from Lupus. She had moved him and her sister back from Los Angeles five years ago when she was first diagnosed with the illness. He was so into his nieces. His sister told Brooklin that her husband died in a motorcycle accident and her baby brother's been nothing but a father to her children. Ray let her know that he felt as though he was surrounded by death. He felt the need to live life to the fullest.

She went to take a shower. Ray invited himself in. They washed each other up and down. Brooklin got out of the shower first. She sat on the bed to dry off. Ray walked into the room and fell to his knees, slowly tasting her insides. He kissed her thighs and she arched her back. His tongue played with her pearl as his index and pointer finger went in and out of her. He rose and eased himself inside. His strokes were gentle as he took his time. As he stroked, she moved to his rhythm and he sucked on her bottom lip. Brooklin held him tightly. He came out and instructed her to turn around. She rose to her knees and he pressed the lower section of her back down as he began to enter her from the back. Holding her by her waist, he pulled her towards him. Ray thrust slowly.

Brooklin laid her head down and slowly gripped the pillow as she gently whimpered and whined. She began to tremble and shake. Losing her balance, she fell. He came hard as she shook. They fell asleep in each other's arms.

Brenda and Angel had some bonding time that didn't occur very often. Angel was astounded when she listened to the stories her mother told her about growing up in a whorehouse. She learned that she had family in Kentucky

As Brenda saturated Angel about her childhood of being raised in a whorehouse, she failed to mention what she found out from her previous doctor's appointment.

Brenda had been suffering from migraine headaches lately. Brenda postponed the doctor and chalked her headache up to stress. The doctor found a bulge in her blood vessel and informed her that it could burst and lead to death at any time. The doctor diagnosed her having a brain aneurysm. He let her know that it could be treated. She would have to undergo surgery that would consist of performing a craniotomy. It would basically expose the aneurysm and close the base of the aneurysm with a clip. He let her know that the surgical clipping remained the best method to permanently eliminate aneurysms. Another alternative was watching her blood pressure, making sure it didn't drop to an abnormal level.

Ray began to fill the void of the unbearable anguish inside that embedded Brooklin. She remained angry with Luther for breaking up their family. Ray was slowly healing her feelings of abandonment she harbored.

Years ago her comfortable and safe world had fallen apart, but Ray was bringing it all back together. Brooklin was haunted by thoughts of C-Note. She didn't know how to express the pain she held deep inside. Brooklin wouldn't allow her inner pain to manifest.

Being devastated by her father's absence, she searched for male affirmation. She craved the love and attention her father had once given her. For so long she felt lost and alone. Vincent gave her the attention she yearned but he lacked the capability to show her the love she thought she needed.

Brooklin was not going to be manipulated. In her confusion and insecurities, she sought pleasure how she saw fit. Ray gave Brooklin the nurturing love that Luther denied her. The affection Ray displayed with her and his family stole her heart.

After four months of dating, Brooklin moved in with Ray. Brenda was able to get back at her routine. That left Angel home alone. Eventually, Reggie moved in. Brenda allowed things that others parents wouldn't, but she lived by a different standard.

Angel figured that was the lifestyle Brenda had been raised in. Brenda's mother had her when she was thirteen. She was the oldest of four children. Brenda's mother was from the Blackfoot Indian Tribe that lived on the Oklahoma reservation. She was kicked off the reservation not only for breeding with a black man but with a white man as well. Brenda's mother was a big disgrace to her family. Brenda's life simply mimicked that of her mother's.

Chapter 12

ANOTHER ONE BITES THE DUST

The Bud and CNC were still at war, going back and forth shooting up each other's block. Each crew was going through desperate measures. They lay in gangways waiting on people to arrive on the block. They even stooped to the level of playing on the telephone. Midnight went to a payphone and called Flintstone's house. His mother became frantic when the operator told her that she had a collect call from C-Note for Ducky. Even B.K. and Clack had been murdered.

Vincent was disoriented by Brooklin's disappearance. When he came home one day, Brooklin had parked the car he had given her in front of his house. He went to knock on the door in search of finding some answers. He caught Brenda coming out of the door.

"Hey, Mrs. Johnson!" Vincent uttered wearing his Tupac fatal attraction look when he starred in "Juice."

"Hello. How are you doing Vincent?"

"I would be doing even better if I knew where

Brooklin was hiding out."

"She isn't hiding. I didn't know what was going on and I didn't want anything to happen to her. I just took her to a place where she could lay low." Brenda talked and walked towards her car.

Vincent followed. "She didn't have anything to be afraid of. She got me!" he said, patting his chest. "I adore her. I worship her. I've killed for her."

Brenda grinned, "Vincent she's okay. I got her. She's been taken care of. Brooklin is in very good hands. I will let her know that you asked about her." She got in her car and pulled off. She was trying to figure out did Vincent say he would kill for her or he had killed for her. She brushed it off.

Angel was in her junior year of high school. It was hard getting up going to school for her. She felt a dire need to stay with Reggie. When she would press snooze, she visualized Harlem. Angel knew he would be so disappointed in her, knowing she came so far and gave up. She couldn't wait for him to call. She wanted to hear all about his college life. When he made his occasional calls, he only got to talk to her. He would ask how everyone else was doing. He even asked about Reggie. She let him know that Brooklin was into a new relationship. The first thing he wanted to know was if Ray was in the streets. Angel let him know that she didn't know very much about him. All she did know was he was supposed to be from California. She had an urge to tell him all that she did know, but her gut feeling provoked her against it.

Ray drove a new two door black 1995 GMC Suburban

with black MB Motoring Bruzer powder coat with the mirror-like machined faced rims. Two days after seeing Ray's truck, Reggie went and purchased himself a black 1995 Chevrolet Tahoe. He didn't drive it until his stereo system and his seventeen inch chrome Antera rims were on the truck.

Ray and Reggie talked when Brooklin and Angel were involved. Reggie was a little intimidated by his presence. He wore IZOD cardigan sweaters, IZOD socks, slacks, polo style shirts, and khakis. When he dressed down, he wore Karl Kani sweaters and shirts with matching hats. His Ralph Lauren jacket was the same color as his Ralph Lauren khakis. He resembled a corporate thug.

Since Ray didn't wear any jewelry, Reggie felt he had one up on him. Reggie had flossed his thick twenty-four inch gold Turkish rope with the gold diamond embedded cross and matching bracelet. When he got his jewelry, he asked the jeweler to make Angel an ankle bracelet with her name on it. The bracelet hit him for eighteen hundred.

Reggie was ready to plant his seed when he found out that Brooklin was expecting a baby. When he sat down to handle business with Vincent, he mentioned it to him. Had he been looking up, Reggie would have seen the rage that filled Vincent eyes.

"Who's the dude she pregnant by?" Vincent asked.

"Some mark ass nigga name Ray." Reggie regurgitated the information so easily. He told him all that he knew except where they stayed and Ray's social security number.

"Is that nigga from L.A.?" Vincent asked.

"I'm not sure, but what made you say that?"

Reggie looked up at Vincent.

"I keep hearing about this dude name LA Ray. He supposed to be a claiming blood or something and he caked up."

"Dude ain't never set tripped with me." Reggie shrugged his shoulders and threw up his Crip sign.

"All that matter is that he is treating her right. Do you have any problems with'em?" Vincent asked like he was really concerned.

"Naw we don't have a problem. He called me this morning to tell me Eazy E died from complications with AIDS." Reggie looked him directly in his face.

"That's fucked up. I heard that too. I damn near cried. I felt like I straight knew dude." Vincent shook his head.

Vincent envied the fact that Brooklin had found a new love, but he was relieved to know that she was happy. He would be there for her no matter what.

Vincent spoke smugly, "Aye Double R, tell me who murked them dudes when y'all went up in that spot."

Reggie looked at him sideways. "Get the fuck outta here! You working with them folks or something?"

"What if I told you I killed C-Note?" Vincent stood up from the table making some powder fall off the scale.

Reggie didn't care about the small amount of residue. He was trying to keep an eye on Vincent. A leery feeling began to fill his body. He was hoping that Vincent wasn't about to try no slick shit. His strap was all the way upstairs.

He chose his words carefully. "I'd ask you why you telling me that shit. Then I'd tell you true niggas never talk."

"So you telling me that you are not going to tell me?" Vincent looked Reggie over.

"Cuz, put it like this. If I tell you, I gotta kill you. What you need to be worried about is trying to make this money stretch like some got damn limos!"

Angel had walked in. A sense of relief fell upon Reggie. She was about to tell Reggie about Brooklin's doctor appointment. When she saw Vincent, she decided to wait.

"Hey, Vincent, what you been up to?" Angel questioned.

"Shit. Trying to maintain. Other than that, everything is everything." Vincent nodded his head.

Reggie stood in front of the stove mixing one gram of baking soda to every seven grams of coke. He shook his glass tube till the mixture was rock hard. Reggie watched as his substance floated towards the top.

"Angel, go get my vest and bring Nina down with you." Reggie turned towards Vincent. "Cuz where you 'bout to go?"

"I'm done for the day. I'm 'bout to hit a couple of corners before I lay it down." Vincent pulled his keys from his jacket pocket. "Where you headed?"

Reggie laid his nine millimeter handgun on the table and put his black bulletproof vest on. "I gotta drop this shit off in the hood to Lay-Loc fat ass."

"Be careful out there." Vincent headed to door.

Reggie waved Nina in the air. "The streets need to be careful. I'm going hard, taking at least three niggas with me. This Bud till I die." He followed Vincent to the door and turned to Angel. "I want you in your birthday suit when I come back!"

"You don't even have to tell me that. This stays tight only for you, baby."

Angel walked to the kitchen and dumped the rubbish from her Philly blunt wrapper in the trash. She opened up the plastic bag, removed the seeds, and then the small sticks. She rolled her blunt and flicked the lighter up and down to dry it up. She ran upstairs to draw up some bath water. When the tub was filled like she liked, she got in and smoked on her herbs.

When Reggie returned, he found Angel just like he asked her to be. Lying on her stomach, he licked up her thighs. She woke up with no problems. Angel spread her legs apart giving him the perfect angle. Reggie rubbed and smacked her ass cheeks. His tongue massaged her anal canal. She flinched and rose to her knees. He bent down under her small frame, with tongue hung out wide and thick, he clobbered her softness. Juices leaked rapidly. He rose to his knees and inserted all nine inches of his thickness inside her.

He stopped himself from reaching his peak and slowly fell on the bed. She slid over on top of him. Angel guided him to her insertion point. He reentered her easily. He raised his bottom from the bed as she glided down his shaft. Moans of pleasure filled the air as he placed his hands on her waist to control her movements. The movements became more intense as he felt his eruption on its way again.

Chapter 13

THANKS FOR MY CHILD

"Girl I wanted to be at that hospital with you!" Angel spat.

"Momma was here and so was Ray. It was three in the morning. I didn't want to wake you and Reggie up," Brooklin spoke slowly.

"I'd told you I didn't care what time it was to call me." Angel.

"Well, in six more months you can call me," Brooklin laughed pointing to Angel's stomach.

"Did it hurt?" Angel whispered.

"Hell yeah!" Brooklin shouted out.

"The fucked up thing about all this: I gotta wobble across the stage with a big ass belly." Angel shook her head.

"I know, but at least you made it. Have you talked to Harlem?"

"Yeah, I told him the date for graduation, but I didn't tell him nothing about me being pregnant."

"I don't know why not. He ain't none of your motha fucking daddy! Let me let you go before you piss me off. You always did do that shit. If Harlem cared about us, he'd have his ass in St. Louis not in Alaska. He just like his got damn daddy. His ass should have been a track star. It's in his blood to run off." Brooklin hung up the phone.

"He in Alabama for your information!" Angel yelled at the dial tone she sat and listened to.

"Reggie, are you going to the hospital with me?" Angel looked at him waiting on his response.

"For what?"

"Brooklin had her babies."

"She did. She named them yet?"

"Yeah. Brandon and Denim."

Reggie looked confused. "Brandon and Denim? Where she get that from?"

"C-Note middle name was Brandon. Where she got Denim from, I do not know. I guess Toni Braxton."

"I'll go with you. When we leave there, I wanna drop some money off to Monica. I haven't been by to see Keena in a while."

"Why don't you pick her up and she can go with us?" Angel suggested.

"I can do that."

The phone rang as they walked out the door. "Why all these damn big ass black crows in our yard?" Angel turned around looking for Reggie's answer.

He went back in to answer the phone. Ten minutes passed and Reggie hadn't come out. She went back into the house. Reggie was slumped down in her chair with a face that was drenched with tears.

"What's the matter baby?"

"Lay-Loc just got knocked. Flintstone walked right up to him as he was about to get in the car with Cent-Dog. The gun jammed when he aimed it at Cent. He took off running. Midnight and Peep-Dog heard the shots. By the time they got outside, he was gone and Cent-Dog pulled him out of the street."

"Baby they shouldn't have moved him."

"It didn't matter. He got up on him and shot him dead between the eyes."

"How many people got to die before y'all realize that shit is not going to end?" Angel asked.

Reggie grabbed his Milwaukee Brewers fitted cap, pulled it down over his eyes and walked out the door. He couldn't stop thinking about his brother. Retaliation was riddled throughout him. Niggas got out of line and he gave them the blues. It was now time to peep game. He vowed Lay-Loc would rest in peace knowing that Flintstone met the same fate. He was about to show his rivals that the 44 Bud was not to be fucked with.

They made it up to the hospital. Brooklin had given birth to identical twin boys. Chubby, chocolate and seven pounds of joy each. Ray stood over at the nursery window pointing out his boys. Reggie had given him a Cuban cigar. He talked to Reggie about the birth as the unlit cigar hung from his mouth.

When they left the hospital, Reggie dropped Angel and Keena off at home. He went to the hood and swooped Peep-Dog. They drove in a black '88 four door Oldsmobile. They sat at the top of the block and waited for any six deuce cat that came.

T-Bone arrived on the block. When he got out of the car, they had rolled up on him and busted several rounds. T-Bone survived after being hit six times.

Every day they felt the wrath. Reggie wasn't going to let them rest. Gunshots became a part of the routine. Like clockwork, before anyone went to sleep, they would hear Reggie's gun bust.

Just like when it all began, they scared the dope fiends off. Flintstone had to set up shop somewhere else. Reggie got pissed that he never saw anyone out. He was destined to find out where they were. He was making sure the murder rate was not about to decline. His loyalty belonged to his hood and making St. Louis the murder capital was his goal. An eye for an eye was his sole answer to any question.

Chapter 14

CAUGHT UP

Angel had graduated from high school and had given birth to a seven pound eleven ounce boy. Reginald St. James, Jr. was born May 11, 1996 at eleven twenty-two a.m. Harlem was there to see the birth of his third nephew. Everything was on time. He came home for the graduation that happened three days before the birth of Lil Reggie.

Reggie knew in his heart it was time to do something different. The lifestyle he was living was bound to cost him not seeing his son coming of age. The game was becoming detrimental for him. Angel's questions constantly rang in his head. He wasn't trying to be judged by twelve nor carried by six. He talked to Angel about them going to Alabama when Harlem left. It was simply just a thought. Reggie never talked about it again.

Angel didn't mind leaving St. Louis. Harlem had told her how slow it was and she may become bored quickly. Angel told him that as long as Reggie was with her, she'd be just fine. He was really afraid of her learning about his chosen lifestyle.

Luther had come up to the hospital. Reggie had been keeping close tabs on him. He knew how important it was to Angel to have him there. When time was approaching, Reggie felt he needed to know where Luther laid his head. He felt obligated to let Luther know when Angel told him how she wanted her father to be a part of the birth of her first child. Luther and Brenda talked and smiled at each other like the love was still fresh.

"What's up with you?" Angel sat in the hospital bed rubbing the thick curly locks on top of her newborn's head.

"I was about to leave and come up there. Brooklin caught me coming out the door. She said Ray got her cooped up in the house and bitches playing on the telephone. Brooklin says she leaving him and them damn kids," Reggie laughed.

"I love her to death, but my sister has serious issues. What she want with you?" Angel looked at the nurse coming into the room.

"She wants me to come pick her up."

"Are you going to pick her up?"

"I told her I was on my way."

"Reggie, I don't think you need to get in between that. Let Brooklin's invincible ass do that shit on her own."

"You right, but I'mma holla at Ray. You want anything before I come back up there?"

"Yeah! Bring me some breakfast from the Sandwich Shop on St. Louis Avenue," Angel requested.

"That's all you want is some breakfast? Baby I'll bring the Sandwich Shop to you."

"Well, got damn me make it happen, but in the meantime I'll take some toast, two scrambled eggs with American cheese, link sausages, and a side order of grits with extra butter," Angel said, giving Reggie her breakfast order.

"What you gonna do with all that damn food? You got to have a high ass metabolism. Anybody else be packing on the pounds," Reggie chuckled. "I'll be up there in a minute. In twenty minutes, call your order in and put it up under my name."

"My damn food bet not be cold!" Angel hung up the phone before Reggie could reply.

Twenty minutes had passed.

"Sandwich Shop. This is Kelly. How may I help you?" Kelly popped her gum the way Flo did on Mel's Diner.
Angel ran down her order and left Reggie's name.
Reggie was coming out his parent's basement. He rode around to the front of the block and saw Midnight by his lonely.

"Whad up?" Reggie raised his chin leaning out the window of his Tahoe.

"You nigga!" Midnight walked around to the passenger side and invited himself in. "Where you headed to?"

"You in now nigga. So it really doesn't matter

now."

They rolled out listening to *Can't Knock the Hustle*.

Heading east on St. Louis Avenue, Reggie stopped at the light. As the song ended and the lyrics settled in, Reggie and Midnight came up out of their daze real quick. Flintstone was scatting across the intersection.

Reggie jumped out of the truck and got all up on him. Shots rang through the air. Bloc! Bloc! Bloc! People on the bus stops were ducking down. Cars were skidding trying to avoid the gunfire. Reggie was walking at a steady pace as he held his Nina pointed directly at Flintstone.

When he hit the ground, Midnight rolled up. "Get in nigga! Hurry up! All the people out here and shit! Who the fuck do you think you are? Scarface or some got damn body?!"

Reggie dropped the truck off and parked it in his parent's backyard. He got in a clucker's car headed to the Sandwich Shop. He was a little pissed at himself. The way he handled that was never is MO. He made a scene and that was the worst thing he could ever do. Now he was thinking that he should have thought about it, but he figured getting to Angel was most important. He didn't have the time to put into following Flintstone's flat footed ass. Believing that that was his only opportunity to get him would eventually cost him some time.

When he made it to the hospital, Angel never uttered a word. She looked at him in his crisp white Stafford T shirt and black denim jeans. He sat the food on the tray and sat in the chair next to the hospital bed. He pulled his black Los Angeles Raiders with the heavy chrome Raiders symbol fitted cap over his eyes.

Angel had lost her appetite. The programming

was interrupted due to the shooting that took place. Bystanders were interviewed speaking how the scene reminded them off the Wild West. They had given accurate descriptions of the vehicle, the driver, and the shooter. The victim was in critical but stable condition.

Angel felt some weakness in the pit of her stomach. She glanced over at Reggie. She didn't mention to him about what she saw on the news. He sat nonchalantly looking at the television. Shortly, he had fallen asleep with his cap pulled over his eyes. He was awakened by his name being broadcasted on the five o'clock news. Reggie got word to the hood to burn up his truck. When his father had paged him, he knew his work was completed. He could only be calling for one or two things. To tell him the truck was on fire in the back of the house or he too had seen the news. He felt there was no need to call him back.

Brooklin called up to the hospital once she saw the news. Her phone call was followed by many. Vincent, Brenda, and Monica were calling to inform Angel of the news they had seen. She was waiting on the phone call from Harlem, but he never saw the news. He was gone before sunrise.

Four months had passed. Reggie was on the run. For some odd reason, he was able to lay low at Angel's house. Brooklin had been home a month. Ray was coming by every day to see his boys and beg Brooklin to come back home. There was nothing drastic taking place in the relationship. Brooklin just took flight.

Things were winding down. Angel had put all of the kids to bed. When she was walking up the steps, there was a knock on the door. As she opened the door, all she heard was "search warrant" being screamed and the house was filled with officers with their guns raised.

Reggie was in the bed sound asleep. The police pulled him right out of the bed. They didn't bother to search the house or anything else. They came for what they wanted. He was escorted right out the door in his blue pinstripe boxers.

Reggie was being arrested for suspicion of having committed a particularly dangerous violent act and belief to be a member of a violent street gang. The St. Louis FBI's top priority was to address and reduce violent crimes that afflicted the citizens that it was sworn to protect. The goal was to rid the streets of the most violent felons. The FBI, St. Louis Metropolitan Police Department, and the Missouri Highway Patrol formed the St. Louis Metropolitan Fugitive Task Force.

Someone had informed the authorities of the whereabouts of Reggie St. James in which they believed he was wanted by the law. Without taking his case to trial, he was sentenced to fifteen years. He would be eligible for parole in seven years.

Chapter 15

Juicy Got' em Crazy

Angel slid on her DKNY jeans and lime green DKNY City shirt. She tucked her shirt inside so that you could see her lime green leather belt that was matching her lime green and black DKNY tennis shoes. As she was about to grab her black leather jacket, the phone rang. She listened as the operator ran the instructions down to her about this collect call she was willing to accept.

"What's up with you?" Reggie asked.

"Nothing. On my way to see this new movie 'Set It Off'."

"That's that movie Queen Latifah in, ain't it?"

"Yeah!"

"Where's my son?"

"He with my momma. She has Denim and Brandon, too."

"Brooklin ain't went back to ole Ray yet?"

"Naw. He still coming by every day. He not even tripping off Brooklin. He just comes to see the kids. Brooklin seems like to have a rush or something, just knowing she in control of that."

"You always said her ass was crazy. She still going around comparing herself to God?"

"Naw. She hadn't said that crazy shit in a long time. Please don't bring that up. She probably come walking in here with that foolishness at any moment."

"How's Harlem?"

"I don't know. No one has heard from him. When I try to call him, all I get is his voicemail every time."

"You talk to Luther?"

"Yeah, he called this morning. He supposed to be going to rehab or something."

"He know I'm locked up?"

"Who doesn't know that Double R locked the fuck up?"
"Do I detect an attitude?"

"No! You asking that shit like your face wasn't on every local channel. Fox, CBS, NBC, motha fuckas was telling me that they saw you on 'America's Most Wanted'. Shit the whole world probably knows. They depicted you to be the resurrected Jesse James the most malicious hood figure today. Do you know how many murders they connected you to?"

Reggie laughed. "Well, gon' get ready for the show. I'll get back at you tomorrow. Love you."

"I love you, too." Angel hung up the phone.

Reggie stood at the pay phone staring amongst the crowd of men that were playing dominos, wondering how long would Angel wait.

Brooklin walked into Angel's room. "Angel, this is Eric. He's going to be hanging with us tonight."

Angel looked the giant over. Standing very tall and very attractive, his caramel complexion seemed to glisten from the shiny glow of his bald head. Angel shook her head because that was not a part of the plan but she went on because she was not about to miss the movie. Her thing was to see the movie as soon as it premiered at the theatre.

The three of them reached the door. Angel opened the door to proceed out and stopped her in tracks. Angel could see the death in his eyes. "Vincent, what the fuck! Why are you just fucking standing there?!!" She wouldn't dare show him her fear.

Brooklin and Eric walked right on past the both of them. Vincent turned to watch them walk away. Angel locked the door and made sure it was secure. She walked past Vincent and he bumped her as she passed.

Angel got in Eric's car. "The nigga is crazy! You betta watch him!"

Brooklin turned around from the front seat of the Blue Beamer. "You just now knowing that? It's like his ass be lurking in the bushes. That shit used to scare me. I wonder how his ass would be acting if I gave him some of this bomb ass pussy!"

They all shared a laugh; even Eric had

something to say, "That shit is the BOMB!"

Brooklin looked at him with the expression of "who asked you anything" before rolling her eyes.

Right after the movie, Eric brought them home. Brooklin got rid of him by telling him she and Angel had some things to talk about tonight so she would catch up with him later. He pulled off not even waiting to see if they made it into the house. Eric had every intention of getting him some ass. He would be back, but she had to call him first.

Vincent met them at the steps before they opened the front door.

"Vincent, why are you always lurking around my damn house?" Brooklin waited on his response.

"I be wanting to talk to you."

Angel shook her head and walked on through the door.

"Brooklin, I wish you could see that your heart belongs to me." The sincerity in his voice was strong.

"How the fuck you figure that?"

"Brooklin, I've loved you ever since we were kids. I have never stopped loving you."

"Vincent, why do you care about me so much?"

He reached out to touch her hair. She had her hair cut so close that he had to eliminate the space between them to caress it. The softness of her hair thrilled him. "I loved you the moment I laid my eyes on you."

Brooklin led him into the house, straight to her bedroom which was two doors down from Angel's. She was in her room listening to the Quiet Storm; she didn't hear them as they passed.

As soon as she shut her door, she undressed. Vincent sat on her queen sized bed, admiring her flawless figure. Unlike Angel, the babies added to Brooklin's figure. Her hips and ass were flawless. Her thickness was just right. Vincent's manhood grew instantly. She stood there waiting on him to make his move. He couldn't believe that he was seeing this. He was about to piss his pants. Breasts were perky, nice and round. They seemed to be staring at him. He was turned on even more by the darkness of her nipples.

"Come get," Brooklin spoke seductively, wiggling her pointer finger.

Vincent was nervous. He wanted to be gentle. The only time he had been with a woman was on occasions when he got with base heads. He talked so dirty to them that the love lost was so evident. Vincent wouldn't dare display that with Brooklin.

He undressed and Brooklin damn near creamed herself. She never knew that Vincent was as buff as he was. He always wore oversized sweat suits that didn't display anything and his tighty whities hid the ten inches he was packing.

He grabbed Brooklin by the hand. She walked over closer to him. He took his time kissing and caressing every inch of her body. He quickly found his treasure. Sounds of pleasure seeped throughout the room. The day he waited for had finally come. It was better than he thought it would be. She would forever be his lady, whether she knew it or not. This was the first night of many more to come.

They laid there and Brooklin poured her heart to him. She apologized for ignoring him while they were young. She didn't have a reason for avoiding him. She just did it. He let her know that it didn't matter because he would wait on her because someone told him if he loved something, let it go. She told him she was afraid to love because her first love ran out and when she began to love again, he was murdered. Vincent asked her about Ray. He saw the twinkle in Brooklin's eye. When she said Ray was heart and mind, he thought he heard his heart break. Ray was her first and she adored everything about him. She just feared him leaving her. She had to depart before he did. Brooklin emphasized that if anything were to happen to Ray, she would take her own life just to be with him.

Vincent held on to every word she spoke. He felt as though Brooklin had given him her heart, but the true owner was Ray. He couldn't take no more. He would settle for the time Brooklin allowed for him. Vincent could never love another. He wanted her so bad to himself. He'd find a way to make that happen but eliminating Ray from the picture wouldn't be the choice.

Vincent cherished all of their conversations. Brooklin had opened up to him. She expressed the hurt that Luther caused her. She was jealous of the relationship Angel shared with Harlem. She even mentioned that she was slightly jealous of the fact that everyone seemed to love Angel more than they seemed to love her, all but their mother. She was now realizing that Vincent showed her more affection than Ray, Luther, or Harlem.

Chapter 16

ALL MY LIFE

"This car is about to break down. I'm not about to put me and my child on the highway in the dead of December just to come see you, Reggie." Angel sat on the side of the bed twirling her feet together.

"Click over and call my daddy." Reggie was getting tired of Angel's back talk. Any other time, she didn't have a problem coming to see him. She had always made him her top priority.

"Call your daddy. I ain't about to ask him to bring me up there. What kinda shit is that? He don't even come see yo ass! Well any who."

"There goes that any who shit. That's just your way of saying fuck what you saying. Angel, would you listen?" Reggie pleaded. "Just call him."

Reggie talked to his father. He told him that Angel was having some financial problems. He reassured him that he wasn't looking for a handout because he had his own. Richard Sr. made him aware that if Lil Reggie needed anything, it would be taken care of. Angel smiled on the fact that Reggie's parents worshipped the ground her child walked on. They made it so evident that they would climb the highest heights for him. Ever since Reggie had gotten himself locked up, his parents picked her son up every other weekend and they didn't miss any holidays.

Reggie informed his father of what he was doing when he was coming and going in and out of the basement. Richard Sr. already knew. He let Reggie know that he would never use it, but he wouldn't give it all to Angel. He said hopefully he could put it to use legitimately whenever he was released from prison. Reggie let him know that Angel needed a new car. His father recommended that it would be in her best interest not to pay cash for it and he would put the car in his name and made sure the monthly payments were made. He would make sure his grandson wouldn't be out on a bus stop or stranded in Reggie's old ass SS.

Angel walked off the lot with a brand new 2002 four door fully loaded grey Acura Legend. Richard had the license and registration squared away. He put a nice down payment on the car and the car note was under $200. It helped that he had A-1 credit.

Brooklin let Vincent know about the new car Reggie had purchased for Angel. He was wondering how Reggie pulled that off from behind bars. Vincent figured he was doing something with money from the capers he had pulled. He went out and brought Brooklin back a 2002 CLK 320 two door grey Mercedes Coupe.

Brooklin was impressed being that Vincent still rolled around in his old school caddy. Vincent had a little change from stacking his chips over the years. He didn't feel the need to floss. He thought low key was the best way. He and Earl remained hustling through the years but they weren't any high profiled cats.

Earl had opened up a liquor store in the heart of the hood. It attracted many because of its high traffic location. This was solely used to wash his drug money.

Angel was turning into the intersection so that she could gas up before her and Lil Reggie hit the highway. A white Eddie Bauer Expedition pulled up to the pump she was headed for. Angel rolled her eyes and went inside to pay for her gas. Kevin followed her in. He was right on her heels as she requested thirty on pump three. When she made it outside, Kevin asked her if he could pump her gas. He looked like Young Jeezy with a T.I. flavor to him.

"Can I pump your gas for you?" he asked.

She looked him over in his blue firefighter uniform. "What you trying to put out the fire that's burning inside of me because you pulled up to the pump I was about to use?"

He looked deeply into her eyes. It was if he was staring into her soul. Kevin was mesmerized with her grey eyes. "You know your car and your eyes are the same color?"

"What kind of lame ass line was that?! I live with these eyes every day. Don't you think I know what the fuck eye color I have?" Angel rolled her eyes even harder.

"Slow up with the CUSSWORDS. I ain't step to y'all sideways." Kevin turned to Angel's car. Lil Reggie was banging on the window telling Angel she forgot his chips and orange soda.

Angel looked at her son seeing nothing but his father. She felt as though she was cheating standing there admiring the figure before her. It had been four extremely long years that she had felt the warm touch of a man. She was determined to be Reggie's personal Winnie Mandela. Her pussy muscles contracted as she stood beside him eyeing his profile while he pumped her gas.

She made it to see Reggie. He strolled in his state issued greys. He had put on weight, but it looked good. She was creaming just sitting there looking at him and thinking of the dude she had just met before coming up there. During her whole visit, she couldn't wait to get to a phone to call Kevin. She was trying so hard to give him a hard time, but he ended up giving her his number. She didn't hesitate to take it.

Reggie talked to his son. They were having the bonding time they only shared when they came to the prison to visit. The first four months of his life was the only time he was free to share the joy of his newborn. Sometimes you could see the hurt in his eyes that he wasn't with his son on a daily basis. He never expressed how he missed him or Angel. She knew that he wouldn't express it. He was too hard for that but Angel saw it in his eyes.

In the beginning when leaving the visit, she and the baby would look back and wave. They eventually stop looking back because the pain was seen in both of their eyes. Tears would well up. So, to prevent each other from crying, she stopped looking back. One day Lil Reggie asked his father why he couldn't come home with them. Reggie was about to breakdown and Angel knew it. She simply told her son that he would be home soon.

She was becoming to dread staying in the motels alone with her son. The drive and the loneliness of the drive were wearing her short. Angel began telling Reggie she was just going to have to see him either on Saturdays or Sundays. She no longer wanted to do both days.

The day she met Kevin, she made an exception. Angel didn't want to drive the two hours rushing to get to a phone and besides she told Reggie she would be back the next day. Instead, she rushed to the room to call Kevin. They sat up on the phone and talked the night away. He thought she lived in Jefferson City, being that was the area code she called from. She let him know that she was visiting her son's father. He wanted to know why he was locked up. She modestly couldn't answer because she felt there was no simple explanation that he was labeled as a menace to society and a task force was designed to rid the streets of people like him.

Angel lay in the bed as her son slept. She was losing the feeling that she didn't want anyone but Reggie. Realizing that she could no longer go without the touch of a man, Kevin had her wide open. She sat up holding the phone and playing footsy while thoughts of Kevin's touch fulfilled her fantasies.

Kevin was a twenty-six year old firefighter. He owned his own barber shop. Kevin rented out six other booths in his shop with three barbers and three beauticians. Things basically paid for themselves.

He worked there on his days off. He worked the C-shift at Firehouse 24. His shift consisted of three days on and four days off. Thursday, Friday, Saturday, and Sunday were his off days. Angel asked him why he was in his uniform this Saturday. He had just attended the funeral of a guy who lost his life in the line of duty from another location.

Angel hated the fact that she would have to wait five more days before she would see him again. She was playing it cool. She settled for the phone calls.

She couldn't believe that he didn't have a significant other. He kept it up front. He let her know that he didn't have a problem making late night phone calls. There was someone on the other end always waiting to receive his call.

Angel had no plans on just being added to his list. She was seeking to be there for a lifetime. For the next eight years, she had become a part of his regimen.

After two months of dating, the time had finally came for the proposition she couldn't refuse. No one was home and Angel was making sure it was going down because no was there to stop her. Signs of lovemaking were all that was going to be heard. Her walls were anticipating Kevin's entrance. She kissed him on his cheek so sweet. He broke her all the way down as he gently beat up her walls. Angel was officially sprung.

The sex was so incredible. The tenderness of Angel's touch was irresistible. That pussy was feeling like new money to Kevin.

Kevin fulfilled all those desires and fantasies she once yearned. That Sagittarius had no limit to where she was taking Kevin. She showed that Capricorn she was so damn sexual doing everything to drive him crazy as she whispered in his ear very seductively. Just like Tyrese, Kevin knew that this was the zodiac freak he had searched for.

Angel's loneliness feeling was gone. The mindset of never finding another like Reggie had disappeared. All her life she had prayed for someone like Kevin and she prayed that he felt the same way.

With Vincent being around all the time, he and Kevin had embraced one another. Vincent was happy because, just like Angel, all his life he prayed to get Brooklin's attention.

Chapter 17

JUST ONE OF THEM THANGS

Lil Reggie, Denim, and Brandon ran into the house screaming, "Granny!" They saw her black two-door convertible Mustang parked in front of the house. They ran straight into the kitchen to hug Brenda. She stood gracefully not looking a day over forty. She kissed her grandchildren. She learned that Kevin had just brought them back from the St. Louis Zoo.

She was so pleased that Angel had chosen someone that was in tune with her as well as her child. The boys would tell her that Kevin was always taking them somewhere. He would cut their hair every Saturday. Ten regulars would come in before he called it a day. He used this as his spending money for the boys. The boys had been up to the firehouse. They would run through the firehouse and slide down the brass fireman's pole. Lil Reggie enjoyed it the most.

It wasn't often that Brenda popped up. She had stopped by to see how the children were doing. She was becoming concerned because no one had heard from Harlem and she was there to express her concerns. She was talking about just going to Alabama to find him. Brooklin changed her mind real quick.

"How you know he wanna be found? That lil' freak

boy is just fine." Brooklin popped her gum loudly.

"Any who, it's only logical for a woman to be worried about her child," Angel intervened. Being that Harlem had never had a girlfriend or no interest in them, his sexuality sat in the back of everyone's head. "I do still have a number where he can be reached. He just don't ever answer the phone. Momma, I'll give to you. You could probably leave him a message on his voicemail."

"I haven't hung out with you girls in so long. Do y'all want to go shopping and grab a bite to eat later?" Brenda asked.

"Yeah! At your expense. You know I'm down for anything when anybody want to spend their money on me." Brooklin patted her chest.

"Let me see if Kevin has anything to do first. He has had the boys all day." Angel evil-eyed Brooklin.

"I'll just call Ray and tell him to come get them. He ain't got nothing else to do." Brooklin called Ray. He let her know once he left the gym he would come pick them up. He already knew that they would more than likely be with Angel or Kevin. Ray had given up on the thought that he and Brooklin would reconcile their differences. He'd date here and now. Ray was fully committed to the well-being of his sons.

Angel and Brooklin had left with their mother. When Ray came by, Kevin let him know he was going to order the fight. Cory Spinks and Zab Judah were going at it. Ray stayed for the fight. When Vincent saw Ray's car staying a tad bit longer than usual, he became furious.

Brooklin's new flavor was Mac Dre. He wasn't white, he was just lighter than light. Pale skin with blue eyes was solely in his possession. His head was shaped like a light bulb. He drove a tan Lincoln

Navigator. Brooklin only attracted niggas that could make things happen, being easy on the eyes was not a requirement.

The phone rang. Reggie was trying to figure out why he hadn't gotten his visit. Reggie knew Angel had started seeing someone. He wondered how long she would be able to hold out. He respected the fact that Angel had someone, but that was not supposed to come between them and what they had.

Kevin listened to the spiel. When the operator was done, he could hear Reggie asking for Angel. He informed him that Angel was out with her mother. Now he respected the fact that she stood him up to be with her mother because that was way out of the norm.

He was trying to figure out the male voice that seemed to be home alone with the boys. He knew Angel had somebody, but he was so unaware of the presence that was filling his void in his son's life.

"May I ask whom I'm speaking with?" Reggie spoke with concern.

"This is Kevin." The confidence was so evident. Ray and Reggie even noticed it.

"Well, Kevin, is my son Lil Reggie there?" The emphasis was strongly placed on son.

There was no answer. The next thing Reggie heard was his eight year old son's voice. He inquired about the person who answered the phone. He knew who all was in the house and he even knew who was about to fight. All he got out of his son was that the voice belonged to "Kevin". Lil Reggie said "Kevin" like his father was supposed to know who that was.

Lil Reggie let his father know that he was going to Los Angeles with Ray when he took Brandon and Denim. He thought about the LA Ray that he once heard of. He had never made the connection. He let it go of his thoughts of asking Ray the connection. He didn't want Ray to know he was partially responsible for Rance not coming through with his supply.

He drifted back trying to figure out the voice that he first heard. The identification of Kevin was unknown. Reggie was no fool. He knew why Kevin was there. When he finished up the conversation with his son, Reggie wanted to speak with Kevin.

Kevin got on the phone. He was confident in where he stood with Angel and Lil Reggie. "Hello." That confidence level was also boosted being that Reggie was where he was. Being denied parole, he would have to do his entire bid.

"Hey Kevin, I just wanna say this. Angel may need you, but Lil Reggie already has a father. He don't need you playing that role because you tapping his momma. She the one that needs you. Feel me!" Reggie waited on Kevin to answer. He was itching for him to say something sideways.

"I feel ya," Kevin smirked. He didn't know nor could care less how Reggie felt. Kevin felt as though if his son meant that much to him, that conversation wouldn't even be taking place because he would be there with his son.

Ray looked at Kevin. "He good people. Double R just got caught up. He was one of those wild ass lil' niggas. He simply thought he was the law. That nigga was a beast."

Kevin didn't let that bother him. He was very secure with himself. He went on to enjoy the victory of Cory Spinks.

Chapter 18

MUST BE NICE

Reggie had gotten in touch with Midnight. Midnight let him know things were all bad around there. The only reason he was there was because his mother wasn't about to move and he had no other place to go. Reggie told him to talk to Vincent for him; he should look out for him. Midnight let him know DA and No Brains was hanging out with Flintstone. They were getting their nose dirty with any and everybody. Peep and Cent Dog barely even came around. They had jobs and shit. If he saw them, it would only be on the weekends.

When Midnight made mention of Tawanna's name, Reggie's radar was on. She had left a number for him to call. He gave Midnight Vincent's information. Vincent got at Midnight real quick.

Reggie talked to Tawanna. For a couple of dollars, she was ready to sell her soul to the devil. She took the bait with no problem. She would be to see him Saturday.

Saturday had approached. She was there bright and early to see Reggie. He looked better than he did the last time she saw him years ago. She let him know that she had three girls by the same lame ass nigga that used to claim to be a blood back in the day. He ran the plan down to her and she let him know that she would be ready next week. Reggie reassured her things would go smoothly. He had a lot of workers that was on his team.

He had everyone from the person who searched the visitors to those that open the doors to enter the visiting room on his team. He would be able to walk straight to the back with the product in hand. Instead of bringing in small packages he would have to swallow, he could get a big enough package he could discreetly tuck in his underwear.

Reggie came up with the plan when he found that a twenty dollar piece of crack sold for $100 behind those walls. The dude that had the business going on in there was small time. He was in a whole other dorm. He talked to him about what was in the making. Reggie set up something so sweet for him he didn't refuse. He only brought him in because he didn't want his thing to go sour. Ole boy went along gracefully and supplied Reggie with some of his people on the outside. He then put Tawanna on those same individuals.

Tawanna would visit both days on the weekend. Her motel would be paid for. She would insert all that could fit inside of her. Even with things sewed up tightly, every jail worker wasn't involved. Things still had to be taken care of discreetly, but the key people were in the right place.

When she entered the correctional facility, she was nervous at first. She had every drug known to man stashed in her vagina. The CO stood at the door as planned. She entered the facility with no problems.

She walked in with her hair in a white girl ponytail. She had packed on a few pounds also, but she was simply thick with it. Her red velour sweat suit hugged all the right places.

Reggie told her never to wear anything so noticeable. People would be looking and watching her. The inmates would eye that fat ass every time she got up.

The transaction went smoothly. Tawanna would go to the restroom and place the items in a place she could easily retrieve the drugs to give to him. Most of the time, she was able to put them in a jacket pocket. Sometimes she would drop them in a bag of chips that he was eating. When the visiting room was packed, she just slid them across the table.

The paraphernalia was wrapped tightly in a thick black balloon-like bag. The drugs would hit the facility before Reggie's visit was over. He would go to the restroom where he had his celly that worked there during visits waiting for him. His celly then had a dude that was waiting on him to move the product. The dope went through so many hands.

After a while, Tawanna had hooked one of her home girls up with Reggie's celly. He was doing double life for killing his aunt and her boyfriend. Tawanna's only involvement came when she was bringing the girl to the prison. Reggie and Tawanna's hands were free from touching the dope. They were just reaping the benefits.

The whole jail was filled with contraband. Sometimes Tawanna would leave the facility with three to five hundred dollars. Reggie would have twenty, fifty and hundred dollar bills folded in the tiniest squares. She had a whole team of wolves within in six months flat. Her aunts, uncles, cousin, and neighbors would have checks from the facility to checks from people on the street coming through. The checks paid for some inmates' drug use.

Reggie had the jail flooded with drugs. He chose this as his past time to make up for the absence of Angel. When his eligibility for parole was approaching, he was going to slow up on all of his activities. Although he didn't have his hand in it literally, he still controlled the happenings of the activity.

Midnight had a team of young goons that were coming up. All those involved on the streets knew there was no getting over. No schemes could ever be made because Reggie could have them touched sitting right in his cell.

Chapter 19

KEEP IT 100

Angel had finally purchased a cell phone for herself. She decided to step out of the dark ages from not having a cell phone. Avoiding being tracked down was her only intention. She pulled up in front of the house, almost afraid to go inside the house because the yard was filled with big black crows.

Getting out of the car and standing inside the car door she screamed. Eventually the crows scattered as she continued to scream. When the last crow was gone, she ran up on the porch.

As soon as she entered the door to the house, the phone rang. The only person that had the number was Kevin and she just knew it couldn't be him because they had just left each other. She bent down to pick up the mail as she answered the phone.

"Hello."

"Angel, do you want to go to Throwback Thursday's at The Broadway? I know how you love that ole school rap and on Thursdays that's all they play." Kevin waited on her response.

"That's cool. You know I don't have anything

to do."

"Did you see about enrolling in those classes?"
Kevin had been sweating her to enroll in her courses.

She had mentioned to Kevin that she always wanted to be a nurse, but she just didn't have the urge. She was comfortable at the time doing nothing because there was nothing she or her son wanted for.

"Kevin, as soon as Monday..."
Kevin cut her off; he didn't want to hear about Monday because it came and went several times. "Well, I have to go meet with this real estate agent about this property. I'll be by there when I am done."

"Okay baby, see you then." Angel closed her cell phone.
Kevin always had his hand in legal ventures. He was about to rent out the two family flat he lived in. He was looking for a house now. He was going to let the two family flat pay the mortgage on his new house.

Angel went to the mailbox and noticed Brooklin had some mail. Somebody was writing her from the same prison Reggie was in. She opened the letter and began to read it.

Dear Brooklin,

What's up? I got your letter and I was happy to know that you are doing okay. Do the right thing for me and stay out of trouble. I know you need and want shit and you know what I am talking about, but if you have to fuck someone just let me no. I won't get mad because I'm a real goon so keep it 100 with me and yourself but just remember that I love you and that I am on my way home.

So have your shit together because I am trying to get rich. Let me know are you with me or what.

I want you to send some pictures of you and the kids. I put some money slips in here. Shoot me some ends.

Now I need to talk to you about some real shit I need you on my side because I ever left your side for nothing and you know that. Now the ball is on you. I have no worry when I touchdown. Don't you worry about nothing now. You know when I was out I was the man and when I get out, I am still going to be the man that I was.

Now dig, I need for you to stay away from those haters out there and don't touch no drugs until I get out. This is real talk. I love you and the kids and let them know daddy is on his way home to them and give them the type of love and support that they need. I am a soldier and a real goon at the same time. So you know better to play with my mind. If you can't wait on me, let me know. Don't miss lead me or lie to me because I wouldn't lie or miss lead you.

Brooklin, you know I need you in my corner, ya hear me. Let me know what the deal is. Either you with me or you against me. I need to know because you are my heart and if you hurt or break my heart, I will never trust you again.

Let me tell you something, I am a real ass nigga and when you met me I kept it real. So either you gone wait on me or not, and I want you to write me and keep me from getting into trouble while I'm in a place like this. I hurt each and every day because I can't see you are feel you. I need you now like you needed me. Keep it real wit a real goon. One love Boo.

Love,
Mac Dre

PS. Send me some pictures of the family and tell them kids I said hi and that I love them.

Angel laughed at the letter and began talking to herself on the way to the trash can. "Real goon, those kids' names are Denim and Brandon and they got a motha fucking daddy. You illiterate bastard. How many times you gotta let motha fuckas know you real nigga? You love some damn kids. Mac Dre yo ass don't even know my nephews. The fuck you talking about you on your way home. Yo ass at a level five camp. Dummy you ain't coming home no time soon!" Angel put the letter and money slips back into the envelope. She was going to give the letter to Brooklin. Good thing it was just sealed with a piece of tape.

Brooklin walked right in as she stood over the trash can. When she walked in the kitchen Angel handed her mail.

"That nigga wrote me back. I just wrote him to see if he had some change lying around. His dumb ass and his friends went into some gay joint and robbed the place. His partner left the keys to the car on the bar and both of their dumb assess went back in to get them. They was high and tripping." Brooklin skimmed through the letter. "That nigga got me fucked up with his real ass. He best find the next bitch to do that bid. Send you pictures of my kids, for what? They got a father. What I look like sending you some pictures? We kicked it for almost six months and that nigga loves me? He was there for me?!" she snapped before tossing the letter into the trash can.

Angel giggled because that was the destination for the letter after she finished reading it, but she figured Brooklin at least needed to know about the letter.

Angel asked her sister did she want to go to The Broadway with her and Kevin. She had the kids squared away. Denim and Brandon were going with Ray and Lil Reggie was going with his grandparents. Their conversation was interrupted when they heard the sounds of Brooklin's car alarm going off. They raced to the window. No one was by the car.

Just as they walked away, Vincent knocked at the door. They both looked at each other. Brooklin went to open the door. He stood in his black sweat suit with the hood over his head.

"Nigga, you look like O. J. Simpson. Where that nigga at you let sleep on the couch?" Brooklin walked away headed back to the kitchen.

Vincent strolled in behind her. He took a seat at the island that sat in the middle of the kitchen. "Brooklin, tell me why you be playing with my emotions?"

Brooklin turned and looked at him with confusion. "Vincent, you get this pussy whenever the fuck I feel like giving it to you. Because you bought me a punk ass Benz, I'm supposed to be yo gal? That ain't how this works. I didn't ask you to buy that damn car." She dangled the car keys in the air. "You can have the mo-tha-fuc-king car back!"

"Brooklin, it ain't even about the car. This is real simple. I have been open-minded about this whole little situation. I let you have kids by another nigga. That hurt me to my heart. That was something we were supposed to share. Since we were kids, I have loved you with all my heart."

Brooklin turned to him. "Look on the real, I don't know what you tripping off of and as far as you 'letting me' have kids by another nigga, you ain't let me do shit! Now I give you some time to get ya mind right. Coming at me all sideways, you make a bitch hate she gave you some pussy." Brooklin walked to the door. Holding the door open, she looked back at Vincent. "You gone head and leave. When I come back from going out, I will give you a call. Hopefully, you'll come to some sensible senses. That's only if you have some."

Vincent didn't put up a fight; he walked out the door. He stared at Brooklin nonchalantly. She wondered what he was thinking but she didn't let it bother her. Once he was out the door with enough room to shut it, she slammed the door. He didn't look back.

Brooklin walked up the steps to her room. She found her something to throw on. She looked in her closet to find some shoes to match the beige and gold Apple Bottom jumpsuit she had on. Grabbing the Gianni Bini shoebox, she remembered her gold wedge heels. She accessorized her outfit with some gold bangles and gold hoop earring that Mac Dre had purchased.

She went to Angel's door. Angel was listening to "Let Me See It" by UGK. She was bent over with her hips gyrating. Her ass and booty cheeks clapped around her purple thong.

Brooklin threw her hands up and snapped her fingers. "Take it off bitch! Bend over let me see it!" Brooklin continued to rap along with Pimp C. Walking towards the mirror, Brooklin and Angel sang and danced to the song. When the song ended, Brooklin let Angel know that she was going to stop by Brenda's before they left to go out. Angel wanted to know why Brooklin was going over there, but she didn't ask. She let her know that once Kevin got there, they would wait on her to get back. Angel told Brooklin that they would be leaving around ten and she needed to be back so they could get there and get some seats.

Chapter 20

THIS IS MUSIC

"Momma, it's me, Brooklin."

Brenda opened the door. She was wearing a heavy cotton crisp white robe with fluffy house shoes. Her hair was cut in a short style similar to the one Angela Bassett wore in "Waiting to Exhale" when she came to grips that her husband had left her for his secretary.

"What brings you by this evening?" Brenda asked as she sat down on her white plush leather sofa.

"Ma, I need a few dollars." Brooklin spoke in a tone that led Brenda to believe she had no other choice but to give it to her.

"What do you need this money for?" Brenda looked at her child, trying to see through her soul.

"You don't need to know all that."

"What the hell? You ask me for my money and you can't tell me what you are going to do with it? Now I am not going to ask you to give it back because I ain't got the money back you borrowed last week and the week before that. The first three times I didn't trip off it. Now you are here for the ninth time. So I need to know what you are going to do with my money!"

"Momma, I ain't got no job. I get a punk ass welfare check and some damn food stamps. Two hundred and ninety-two dollars don't get me through the month. The only reason I asked is because I am going out with Angel and Kevin. I don't wanna go nowhere broke." Brooklin began to pout.

"Looks to me that you don't need to go anywhere." Brenda folded her arms. "I know damn well that as long as Angel has a couple of dollars, you have a few of dollars. So, needing money to go with Angel is not working for me."

Brooklin and Brenda went into a screaming match. Brooklin let out every bit of hate she had been holding for years. She told Brenda how she wasn't any kind of mother. She pointed out everything she felt Brenda had done wrong. She even mentioned how wrong she was for choosing a drug addict to date and then have children with him. Three kids at that.

She had given Brenda a piece of her mind. Brooklin had gotten so loud that one of Brenda's white neighbors came and knocked on the door to see if everything was okay. Brenda got rid of him by letting him know that they were having a mother and daughter quarrel.

When the neighbor left the door, Brenda gave Brooklin a piece of her mind. She let Brooklin know she was just as bad as her. She told her how Ray was the best thing to ever happen to her. Had she stayed with him, she wouldn't be at her house begging for money. She drove it in the ground how stupid she was for walking out on him. She let her know that, just like her own father, she left whatever they were both afraid to face head on. "Two stupid motha fuckas" was what she called Brooklin and Luther.

Brooklin hearing that made her realize she possessed ways like her mother and father. Brooklin stormed out of her mother's apartment. She tried to close the door but as hard as she slammed, it popped back open. Brooklin's car peeled off leaving tire marks on the pavement.

She had cried and talked herself all the drive back to her house. When she pulled up, Kevin and Angel sat in his truck waiting on her. Brooklin got out running in the house. Kevin blew his horn to let her know they were in the truck. She let them know she had to go clean her face and she would be right back outside. It took Brooklin approximately fifteen minutes before she came back outside.

Kevin stepped out his Expedition. He straightened up his grey black designer Enyce sweater with pink splattered on the front that he wore over a white, black, blue and pink plaid button down. His black Enyce jeans were creased with heavy starch. The point of his crease landed in the center of his white on white Air Force Ones.

Angel strutted alongside him sporting a skin tight Parasuco denim jean jumpsuit. The hot pink fur vest set the outfit off as it matched the hot pink Baby Phat stilettos. Together Brooklin, Angel and Kevin walked in The Broadway looking like new money.

The Broadway was packed. DJ AJ was doing his thang. He was mixing Ice T's *6 In The Morning* track over Rodney O & Joe Cooley's beat *Everlasting Bass*. Throughout the night, you heard every eighties cut there was.

Brenda went to the door as she heard the knocking. Not bothering to see or ask who it was, she opened the door and turned and walked away. "You done cooled down now and you come back to apologize?" When Brenda realized her question was going unanswered, she turned to see what was taking who she thought was Brooklin so long to answer her question.

"What brings you by here? Now you have never popped up over here before?"

On the way home Angel was telling Kevin how glad she was that he told her about The Broadway. "Now that was rap music. I ain't with all that commercial rap. I know all our music wasn't really nothing you could dance to but if you put it to beat like he did. Shit! You can dance to anything!"

Kevin felt her. "That music nowadays doesn't really represent hip-hop. The lyrics in these songs don't state nothing. It's just has hooky beats and chorus lines. I wanna hear music that has meaning. You know shit like that old shit LL used to spit." He cut up the "Breakthrough" album by L.L. Cool J and the lyrics of "The Do Wop" vibrated and rattled the windows. On the ride home, Angel thought about how much Reggie would have enjoyed that.

Chapter 21

DILEMMA AT MY PLACE

When Kevin pulled up to the house, he couldn't get the regular parking space directly in front of the house. A police cruiser was occupying that space for the moment. Angel looked up and saw two officers walking from the porch.

"Excuse me? Are you looking for someone that lives here?" Angel pointed towards their house.

"Yes. We are looking for Brenda Johnson's next of kin. All of her emergency contacts are believed to live here."

Brooklin hopped out the truck, hearing the tallest officer. "That's our mother. Is she okay?"

"I am sorry to inform you that a few hours ago your mother was discovered brutally murdered. There was no forced entry. We are assuming that she knew the perpetrator." The officer reached out to catch Brooklin before she passed completely out.

Angel felt weak. Kevin held her as he walked her into the house. Both officers followed with Brooklin. The paramedics were called. After Brooklin came to, Kevin drove them to the precinct. Someone was needed to identify the body.

Angel looked at Brooklin. She knew Brooklin was

not going to be capable. Kevin let Angel know he was willing to identify her. She let him know that she just wanted him by her side as she entered the room.

Before she walked in, she tried to call Harlem. After calling several times, she decided to go ahead a leave a message. She was totally against letting him know that their mother had been murdered over an answering machine. She had no other choice. She hoped that he would finally return the call knowing that such a tragedy had taken place.

Angel walked in and the examiner had Brenda lying out in the center of the room. When she pulled the sheet back, Angel wept out a loud sigh as she fell back into Kevin's arms. He embraced her tightly. She nodded assuring the medical examiner that was her mother.

Once the relatives were notified, the news stations were now at liberty to release the victim's name. Luther sat and watched. He wasn't sure if that was his wife due to the fact that the area she lived in was predominately white. He was not aware that Brenda had long ago moved away from his children. Just as he was about to turn the channel, her picture came across the screen.

He ran out and gotten himself so high. Luther was drowning all his sorrows as he sucked heavily on the glass pipe. He was ready to join Brenda, but it wouldn't be that night. Two years clean and waiting on the day he was able to go back and be with his family. Luther had backslid.

Harlem listened to the message. He played it several times. His wife wanted to know what was wrong. She dared not ask because he was so secretive. She would wait on him to let her know. She felt a little at ease when he told her to pack because he had to go home for a couple days.

Reggie was calling to make sure his package was coming through straight. He didn't receive any answer. He called Midnight. Midnight let him know that Angel's mother had been murdered.

"Man, they say the perpetrator struck her in the head with a blunt object and a blood vessel erupted and she died instantly." Midnight shook his head.

Reggie hung up to call Angel. After not getting an answer, he called his father. His father let him know that his son was with him. He hadn't heard anything and he intended to go by Angel's. He would keep Lil Reggie with him until things were worked out.

Brenda never did the surgery for the aneurysm and the blow from the object instantly killed her.

Chapter 22

IT'S SO HARD TO SAY GOODBYE

Reggie sent a sympathy card to Brooklin and her boys, to his son and to Angel. He had flowers delivered to the house and he also had them delivered to the funeral home. He wished he could be there for Angel in her time of need. This was the day that he realized it was time for him to get his shit together so he could get his ass home. He was just about done with his last package and he still hadn't gotten in contact with Vincent.

During the processional, Harlem came in with his wife, Ellen. She was a photogenic carbon copy of Sharon Stone. It was evident that she came from money. Her flawless skin and perfectly white teeth were evident.

Behind the couple were Kevin and Angel. Kevin looked as if he had come from a photo shoot. He profiled prolifically in his black Armani tailor made suit. Angel wore the exact same black Donna Karan pantsuit that Brooklin wore. When she went to get her and Lil Reggie something black to wear for the funeral, she just picked her sister out something just in case she didn't have any appropriate funeral attire.

Luther walked in holding on to his grandson,

Lil Reggie. Kevin had picked him up the day before to take him to the store so he could get a suit. He had picked up weight since he stopped smoking. His skin looked soft as butter. After leaving the mall, Kevin took him to the shop to give him a fresh haircut.

Brooklin walked in with Vincent. Ray was right there behind them with his sons. Ray assumed Vincent was there to support his childhood friend. Brooklin had never mentioned to Ray the past that she and Vincent shared. His black Brooks Brother suit showed off his masculine physique.

After the processional was over, the pastor read the scripture of Psalm 23. The choir started off humming and then quickly singing "Jesus is on the mainline telling him what you want."

During the condolences, people from Brenda's job spoke. Her estranged lover spoke of the good qualities that she provided the company for many years. He told the family if there was anything that they needed to not hesitate in calling him. He came out his pocket for the services. He made sure that Brenda was put away in the best. The casket alone was ten grand. It was a rose pink trimmed in rose gold. She had a hefty insurance policy but he wanted the children to receive all of it.

Nearly everybody that they had grown up with was there. Ruth and Rachel made an appearance. Nita, Nikky, Joe-Joe, and Lil Charles sat with the family. Toni was with her husband. He played professional football for the New England Patriots.

When the pastor asked if there were any more speakers, Brooklin stood. She walked to the front of the church. "Harlem and Angel, God makes no mistakes, but this time I am wondering did he or am I just being selfish?" Pointing to her seat, she continued. "As I sit over there, I still can't believe this." She turned to the casket. "Ma, the time has come and you have left me. I thank God to be your child. You gave me life as you guided me and encouraged me to stay on the right path. You showed me the strongest level of independence there is up until your last day on this earth. It has not sunk in just yet; this is simply me saying that Momma, I will see you later because I will never tell you goodbye."

The choir soon sang *His Eye Is on the Sparrow*. They rocked the church. This was truly a home going celebration. The eulogy couldn't be read in complete silence because the sounds of everyone weeping filled the air. After the parting view, the family was led to the limos.

The interment took place at Jefferson Barracks National Cemetery. Being that she and Luther were still married, she was able to be buried where the military reserved the gravesite for its fallen soldiers. The repast took place at the family's home.

Auntie had cooked up a slew of food. Everything was from scratch. Thanksgiving had passed and Christmas was on its way but in between they had a feast in representation of both holidays. The desserts hit all the right spots. Everyone wanted to know how much time it took and when did she find the time to cook all the food. Candied yams, turkey and dressing, macaroni and cheese, banana pudding, Rum cake, and mostaccioli scents filled the air. People ate until they hurt.

Auntie had a way with the kitchen. It was so strange that she was still right next door. Everyone still graced the homes that they once resided. They had grown apart. This day, that broken bond went unnoticed. It's so strange how death can bring people together.

Harlem walked in and looked around. He was impressed with the contemporary furniture that the girls had updated the house with it. He couldn't get over the fact that his mother was gone. He was shocked that no one asked him about his wife. Harlem was really trying to keep his wife out the way of Brooklin. He knew Angel wouldn't have much to say; it was Brooklin he was worried about.

Harlem talked with Luther. He told him that the law firm he worked for was the most respected in the state. If he didn't make partner soon, he was looking to work for Kellogg with a salary of two hundred fifty thousand a year. He did the majority of the talking because Luther sat in a deep depression. He wanted to let Harlem know he was proud of his accomplishments in his career. He avoided it because he didn't want him to bring up his past or anything else that would take the focus off the mourning of Brenda.

Lil Reggie, Denim, and Brandon entered the room. Harlem was trying to figure out the difference to the twins. He didn't know them apart. Lil Reggie let him know which was which. Ray came in and gave Harlem a handshake. Then Kevin introduced himself.

Vincent sat off in the distance. Brooklin had brought him a plate and a glass of water. He thanked her and sat his items on the floor beside him.

Ellen walked into the kitchen, asking Angel if she needed help with anything. Brooklin gave her the nastiest look. "Tell me why the fuck are you here? You with my brother because he's a big shot lawyer in Alabama. Do all you Alabama whores stalk all the prominent black men? I didn't get your name. You been up in this house and tucked away in a room. Did Harlem tell you he was ashamed of us? If I have to say so myself, he picked a nice one. All my life, I thought my brother was gay. I'm relieved to find out his into women. You couldn't convince your husband to bring you to meet his family? I guess it's all true; white women are just as weak as people say they are. That why these black self-righteous niggas run out and get them a white woman!"

"Are you finished?" Ellen asked with a straight face.

Harlem stood in the shadows. He tapped Ellen on the shoulder. He told her to get her things. He kissed Angel on the cheek and told her to call him. He went to say his goodbyes to the rest of the family.

Angel looked towards Brooklin, "Happy now."

Chapter 23

TIP DRILL

The night that Brenda's untimely death crossed the television screen, Luther had engulfed himself with the best drugs money could buy. That was the last time he had been high. It was time for him to take the stand and be the man he sought to be in the first place. He moved in with his daughters. Brooklin tried to move him in Brenda's room. He refused. The two weeks he stayed there he and Brenda shared so much. The memories were still fresh.

The room was different. Brooklin had converted it into a boy's room. Everything that represented a boy was there. Luther chose Harlem's old room. That inconvenienced Lil Reggie He didn't mind because he spent most of his time in Brandon and Denim's room.

Brooklin was glad to have him around. She didn't express her happiness verbally, it showed through her actions. She fixed him breakfast and dinner every day. She would sometimes convert into her childish ways. Luther would smile when he woke up and saw Brooklin curled up under him.

The Fourth of July was three days away. Angel wanted to drive to Sikeston to go to Boomland and get some fireworks. Kevin told her that they could go that morning. He didn't want the boys trying to pop their fireworks without adult supervision. He knew they would grow impatient with fireworks and waiting to pop them.

Angel was becoming overwhelmed. She was working closely with the people investigating her mother's murder. She wanted to ask Brooklin what happened the night she went over there. She remembered that Brooklin had on beige and there was not an ounce of blood on her outfit.

When the investigator let her know that blood was all over the place, she knew it couldn't have been Brooklin. Her lover was away on business in Italy. He was the prime suspect but he had a valid alibi, so that ruled him out.

Ray had called Kevin up to see if he wanted to hang out. Kevin obliged. He went to ask Luther if he wanted to hang with him and Ray. Luther let him know that he hadn't been out in so long that a crowd of people would probably scare him. Kevin let him know he would be okay. It didn't take long to convince him to come along.

Kevin ran to the mall to pick him and Luther up some gear. When he showed Luther a Sean John denim jacket and jean outfit, Luther smiled. He was so glad he had cleaned himself up. He was enjoying life now. He just wished that Brenda could see him.

Ray walked in with a Ralph Lauren blue plaid cardigan sweater with heavily starch blue khaki Ralph Lauren pants. The dark brown Polo boots matched the dark brown plaid designs in his sweater. His rose gold Cartier frames tilted from his nose as he glanced around the scene. Kevin swayed his masculinity in his Rocawear with Luther following behind. Ray received daps and hugs as the trio walked into the Pink Slip.

The Pink Slip was a shake joint in East St. Louis. This is the place where you can find bitches with bullet wounds. There were no hiring requirements and everything goes. Poles were spread throughout the place with women twirling on them.

Luther was amazed with all the ass and titties he saw walking through the place. He leaned in to Kevin. "I need to speak to the manager. He needs to get some better looking broads in here with their titties sagging and stretch marks. Dem hoes need to cover that shit up!"

They noticed Earl sitting at a table with three other men. All four of the men were making it rain. Their table was flocked with women. Earl really didn't know Ray, Kevin, and Luther but he knew about them from Brooklin and Angel. Earl had always been cordial and spoke when he saw any of them. Earl sent them a round of drinks.

Ray laughed. "These niggas be spending that money on these chicks. They got a couple of bad bitches though. You'll see them when they come out to perform."

"Shit they better hurry up before I go sit my old ass in the car." Luther waved for the waitress.

Kevin ordered three Coronas. He let the young lady know she could set him up a tab. As long as they didn't have to sit with empty bottles, she would be taken care of.

Ray laid a bunch of ones on the table. Kevin had gotten change for a hundred dollar bill. Luther looked at the both of them. "Give me some damn pennies. These bitches ain't worth a quarter."

"Passion to the stage!" DJ AJ repeated several times. When Passion graced the place with her presence, the crowd went wild. Luther bucked his eyes. Nelly's "Tip Drill" echoed through the Pink Slip.

Luther had set his eyes on the baddest bitch. He admired the round perkiness of her breasts. The ass spoke measures. The kind of ass Sommore, the comedian, dreams of. You know the one so big you can sit a drink on it. Luther grabbed the dollar bills off the table and walked to the stage. "Here ya go chocolate drop." Luther was making it rain, in his mind anyway. If he had a thousand ones, she was getting them all. He signaled for her to bend down. He whispered, "How old are you?"

With passion in her voice, she told him she was twenty-two. He walked away.

Ray looked up with a smile, "What's wrong ole dude?"

"That damn girl younger than my baby. Her daddy needs to beat her ass." Luther shook his head. His daughters weren't really doing much with their lives but he was sure in the hell glad that they weren't degrading themselves for a few dollars. He was now ready to go. He leaned toward Kevin. Getting right up in his ear making sure he could hear him, "Got damn me. Tell me what the fuck they putting in the milk. These girls got bodies like some real grown women!"

Ray was admiring Passion. She was the reason he wanted to pay the Pink Slip a visit. Passion was a cornbread fed chic. She was from Decatur, IL. She drove to St. Louis on the weekends just so her family and friends wouldn't know what she did for extra money. Passion would make five grand flat.

Ray had met her when she was coming to the gym. She had come through with another dancer. Ray couldn't continue working out. He stopped doing what he was doing and focused on Passion. When she noticed he was seducing her with his eyeballs, she walked over to him. She dropped a card on him.

They had talked on the phone a couple of times. He thought he was sweet talking his way into getting some pussy but Passion wasn't easy at all. He talked and she talked. He made advances to get her to come over. He even tried meeting up with her. Impressing her with his money got him nowhere. She was not coming up off anything. Ray wanted to know if she had a "lick her" license. He couldn't deal with rejection. It had never happened to him before. Most women threw pussy at him.

Kevin laughed. He was starting to enjoy the time he spent around Luther. Kevin had lost both of his parents in a house fire. He was twelve years old at the time. His parents were celebrating their fifteenth anniversary. Kevin had begged them to let him stay home alone.

When they came home, Kevin didn't hear them. His father was making his wife and himself some coffee. He laid a cloth towel on the stove. The pot and the towel had burned. His parents' bedroom was right by the kitchen. When the kitchen had burned, the bedroom soon followed. Kevin heard the smoke detector and ran outside. The fire trucks were in route. When the fireman arrived, they asked him if anyone was in the house. He shook his head no. It was too late when he looked down the street and saw their car. When the firefighters discovered the couple, it was too late. They were burned beyond recognition.

Chapter 24

LOVE DON'T LIVE HERE ANYMORE

Reggie had called and called. No one was picking up the phone. Angel had been looking at the caller ID the entire time. She did not want to talk to him. She had written him and thanked him for the cards and the flowers. There was no pertinent reason she was not answering the phone. She didn't even know why she was avoiding his call.

Angel snatched the phone up not saying hello she listened to the pre-recorded message. "Hello."

"Hi Angel."

"Hi Reggie."

"Is my son there?"

"He will be here tomorrow. We are going to get fireworks. Your father just came to get him about an hour ago. He told me that he and your mother had been to see you."

"Yeah. They brought my son up here weekend before last to see me, since you can't bring him."

"He told me."

"Did he tell you what I said?" Reggie inquired.

"No! What did you want to tell me?"

"I love you and I'm coming for what's mine!" Reggie waited for her to object. "Hello. Are you still there?" Reggie asked.

Angel let him know she was still there. She held the phone and listened to him talk. He started off by telling her he had nothing against her. He was just a little disappointed in her. He had known eventually that she would become involved with somebody; he just thought she would still be there for him. He questioned why his calls went unanswered. Expressing how she played him, he reiterated that there were no hard feelings.

Fair exchange, no robbery was the way he put it. He left her alone. The silly choices he made put her in a situation he could not prevent.

Angel let him know that she still had love for him, but she wasn't in love with him. She talked about thinking about enrolling in college. She decided it was time to make something of herself. All her life, people had looked out for her. She never accomplished anything on her own. She wondered how she would have survived had she had to do it all by herself.

Reggie asked about everybody when their two hour conversation was coming to an end. She told him that Harlem had married a white woman and all he hung around was white people. They shared a laugh because they thought his disappearance had something to do with his sexuality.

Before he hung up the phone, he wanted to know was Angel in love with Kevin. Angel mentioned that they had been together for seven years now. She went on by telling him about the relationship that Kevin had formed with her father, her nephews, and their son.

Listening to her, he felt that there was still a chance. Then she broke it down to him slowly. Kevin had closed on his new home a couple a months ago. He had purchased a five bedroom house. While they were there, he told her that the house was big enough for her, Lil Reggie, and the children they would share.

He got down on one knee and asked her to be his wife. She looked at the four carat platinum ring as she told Reggie the details.

She knew that Reggie didn't want to hear it, but she had to be the one to tell him. She took the ring without verbally telling him yes. Kevin seemed fine with the head nod, the smile and the tears. In the back of Angel's mind was the love she still had for Reggie. She wanted to say yes. But, she felt she still needed to give Reggie a second chance.

Chapter 25

EVERYTHING THAT'S OLD GET TOLD

Vincent looked through his rearview mirror. He watched the officer as he approached the driver side of his car. Vincent was being stopped for a minor routine traffic stop. He failed to display license, registration, and proof of insurance. In all the years of his life, he had never been pulled over let alone questioned by an officer.

Just as the officer was about to walk away, he noticed the Mossberg pump that Vincent had laying on the backseat of his car. Vincent showed no sign of guilt. The officer asked him to step out of the car. Vincent did as instructed. When the officer asked him about the Mossberg pump, Vincent's expression showed that he was just as surprised to see the gun as the officer.

He was arrested. The car was impounded and the Mossberg pump was confiscated. Vincent didn't say a word. He was booked, fingerprinted and processed. His luck had run out. His prints turned up to be a match for a suspect that they were trying to locate. Fingerprints had been lifted off the blunt object that was used to murder Brenda. His fingerprints matched those that were found.

Vincent underwent a series of questions. There

was no game of good cop versus bad cop taking place. Brenda's estranged lover was well connected in St. Louis. He made sure Brenda's case remained opened.

Vincent concocted a story about how he sat in the car and waited on Brooklin to come back from her mother's apartment. He said that when he reached the apartment, Brooklin was beating her mother with a piece of the tall floor lamp that was opposite of the front door.

Kevin pulled up in front of the house. The boys hopped out. The night was approaching and they couldn't wait to pop those fireworks.

Kevin started up the grill. Angel brought out the meat she had seasoned the day before. Luther was in the backyard doing his thing. He thought Kevin was going to barbecue. He told them that had he known his services would be rendered, he would have started early.

When Ray walked into the backyard and saw Luther standing in front of the grill, he laughed. He began to tease him as he stood in his apron and big chef hat on. Ray told him he was going to make a beer run and he'd be back. Luther yelled he should have brought the beer when he knew he was coming. He thought Kevin had taken care of that.

Luther hated this holiday. He never came outside on this day. Usually he was asleep. The sounds of the fireworks gave him flashbacks of the war.

The night was coming to an end. Kevin was watching the boys closely, making sure no mishaps were going to happen. He knew there was nothing that he could prevent, but he was doing his best making sure the boys handled the explosives carefully. Brooklin had left right before it was time to clean up the mess. This wasn't nothing new. She always ran when it came time to do some work.

Everyone was cleaning up as the police cruiser pulled up. Both officers exited the car. They were looking for Brooklin. Kevin sent the kids into the house. The officers informed Angel that there was a warrant out for Brooklin's arrest. Angel lost all composure when she heard them say she was wanted for questioning for the death of their mother.

Brooklin had pulled back up in front of the house while the police were still there talking with Angel. She only came back for a change of clothes. She was handcuffed and taken to jail.

She was wishing she had never came back to retrieve those items. Brooklin knew there was a misunderstanding. She just didn't have the energy to fight.

Chapter 26

PARTY ALL THE TIME

"Hey Daddy. I'm going to go out for a couple of hours. Is it okay if Lil Reggie stays here with you?" Angel asked.

"Now girl you know that you don't have to ask me that. Where are you going? Back to that damn Broadway place?"

"Yeah. A friend of mines I went to school with named Teresa meets me there every Thursday."

"You got friends from school?" Luther toyed with Angel.

Angel twisted her eyeballs. "Dad, I know a lot of people from school. Teresa is just there all the time. She likes the ole school music they play just as much as I do."

"Why isn't Kevin going with you?"

"He'll be over later. He has been working on the house he bought."

"He not trying to take you away from the ole man. I noticed that nice rang on your finger. You wanna tell me about that?"

"Did Kevin put you up to this?" Angel asked with irritation.

"Well, Angel, he did. He wants to know when you are going to give him an answer. I don't understand why you got the rang in the first place."

Angel got dressed and called Ray to let him know that she was leaving and, if he has something to do, Luther was there with Lil Reggie.

The place was packed. Kyjuan from the St. Lunatics was having his regular lime green party. Everybody in the club had on a shade of green. Nelly, Murph, and Ali with his heavy starched creased up jeans was in the place looking like brand new money. After every other song, people were yelling the infamous "Derrty ENT! We all we got!" DJ AJ played all the Lunatic's records on ole school beats.

Angel weaved and wound her body through the crowd. She had tried to call Teresa's cell phone. She figured she was there and, with the loud music, she would never hear a phone ring. Just as she was about to walk around the place for the third time, Angel looked towards the VIP and saw Teresa waving her hands.

Angel walked up the steps. It was a lot cooler at the top than it was in the crowd down on the lower level of the club. When "Country Grammar" came on, the crowd was in Nellyville. The whole place was rapping. The loudness drowned the speakers. If there were any Nelly haters in the place, they didn't want to come out to play the hate game tonight. It was evident that the love was there. DJ AJ put Nelly on blast, "Nelly, you got them ends you can lend ya friends now?"

The night was winding down. Angel let Teresa know she would call her tomorrow. She walked through the crowd. Dudes were reaching and grabbing to get her attention. She wrapped her ponytail around the rubber band to get it off her neck. She felt a reach that wouldn't let go. She turned around and saw Midnight. Angel turned back to give him a hug. He walked her out to her car. He let her know that Reggie had gone up for parole and should hear something by December 6th.

She remembered when Reggie had snatched out on the fifteen, he would be eligible for parole in eleven years. Dealing with Kevin had totally taken her mind off Reggie. She didn't realize that that much time had slipped away. Angel made a mental note that she was going to enroll in those classes first thing in the morning.

Morning came and Angel was at the admissions office at St. Louis Community College. She was looking to enroll in the nursing program. She was informed that there was a waiting list because the program was currently full. She was allowed to take prerequisites until the time allowed her to join the nursing program.

When she came home, Kevin had a surprise waiting for her. He didn't know what made her do it, but he was glad. And it wasn't even Monday.

Kevin called the house and told Angel to come outside. He was sitting in a burgundy 2007 BMW 135i Coupe.

"Damn derrty! You doing it like this?!" Angel grabbed the car door.

"Naw derrty. You doing it like this. This is my expression of gratitude for you in taking your first step."

"Damn can I get an Aston Martin when I graduate?" Angel kissed him, hugged him, and embraced him tightly. He was going to get some special loving tonight.

Ray pulled up and the twins hopped out of his Escalade. They ran into the house. Ray parked and walked over to the BMW. "This is nice. This you man?"

"Naw. I got this for Angel." Kevin looked at the car.

"Damn you cutting that much hair and putting out that many fires!" Ray gave Kevin some dap.

Ray joked with Kevin. They had several conversations. He knew that he was left with a couple dollars that would set him straight for the rest of his life, if he played his cards right. Kevin was investing in any and everything. He even had Ray investing his money into some legal ventures.

Angel was fighting some temptations. With thoughts of Reggie re-entering the picture, she was now willing to see an alternate path. However, her being open minded was about to create problems for her and Kevin. Allowing extra time to analyze the situation meant wasting valuable energy. She doubted anything would be possible with her and Kevin. Trying to remain true to her inner feeling was taking her overboard. She didn't know whether Reggie was coming home, but the possibility that he was weighed heavy on her.

Chapter 27

TAKE THAT SHIT TO TRIAL

Everyone was getting ready to attend Vincent's arraignment. The prosecuting attorney had talked with Luther and let him know that Vincent was looking to plead guilty and wasn't going to take things to trial.

Luther, Kevin, Ray, and Angel were in attendance. Ray's sister had his children and Lil Reggie was with his grandparents.

The judge went over Vincent's charges. He was charged with 1st degree murder, 1st degree assault, and 1st degree burglary.

The judge allowed the family to speak to Vincent. Angel went first. Vincent held his head down as she began to talk. "Vincent, I just want to know why you felt as if you were God and thought it was left up to you to determine how much time my mother had left on this earth. I can't bring myself to understand. You were at our house damn near every day. My mother cooked for you. You at our dinner at our house. She was nothing but nice to you. Even when you tried to date her daughter, she never shoved you away. When I found out that it was you and you are trying to say that Brooklin assisted in the bullshit, I knew your ass was crazy. But I know exactly what this is all about. My mother took Brooklin from you and you didn't know where to find her. You a real shady ass dude! You are truly selfish! I bet you thought this would bring you and Brooklin closer together. Vincent, look at me you lousy motha fucka. Talk bastard! Explain yourself! Tell me why the fuck you took my mother from all of us!" Angel broke down and started to cry.

Kevin walked up to bring her back to her seat. When Angel was seated, he walked up to the podium. "Vincent, man I just want you to know that Brenda was this family's matriarch. You took her away from her grandsons. She will never get to see her daughters get married. You took that from her. That woman would have given you her last. Whatever the reason, was it worth you killing her? If you cared for Brooklin so much, why would you hurt her like this? Man, I know how my woman is over the feeling to a certain extent. See, I know what it is like to lose your mother, but to lose her the way Angel lost hers, I can only imagine. You betta hope God forgives you for this sin!"

Ray was sitting there trying to sink all this in. He envisioned Vincent trying to take his life over Brooklin. In all the years he had seen Vincent, he had no clue that he was that obsessed with Brooklin. He sat on the bench thanking God that Vincent spared him and his children.

Luther walked up to the podium. "In 1972, I entered a food joint and there stood my future wife. She was looking beautiful as ever. She had dreamed to come to St. Louis and take this city by storm. I robbed her of that. She was looking to be something because she was already somebody. She gave me three beautiful children. I wasn't the man that I was supposed to be. I got out in these streets and started tripping. I left her to raise our children. I thought she hated me for leaving, but every time I came around, I could see the potential that she saw in me. I knew that once I let her know I was ready, my love was going to let me return and do the job I was meant to do, but you took that opportunity from me. I want you to know I am not mad at you. Although my daughter is getting a raw deal for what you did, I'm still not mad at you. But got damn me I hate yo ass and you better be lucky they caught yo ass before I did. I already ran out on my kids, but if it wasn't for my grandkids I would take that Sheriff's gun and kill yo ass dead right now! You sorry mother fucker you!" Luther had snapped. The sheriff that was closer to him placed his hand on his gun. The judge looked around to the other five Deputy Sheriffs.

Angel and Luther went to go see Brooklin. They let her know that Vincent was sentenced to life without parole. For a moment they cried together. Luther said a special prayer for Brenda.

Angel and Luther took turns with the phone receiver. Angel now had the receiver, "I am going to write a book about my life. This shit is going to hit the best seller's list in no time! Oprah gone be calling my ass real quick. I just don't know why that boy would do something like that!"

Brooklin looked into Angel's eyes, "I be in that damn cell trying to figure that shit out. I can't believe I'm still sitting here and my bond is secured. I ain't even did shit. Do you know how many motha fuckas in here on lockdown for shit they didn't do?! This justice system is a bitch. That nigga Vincent. Man." Brooklin shook her head and tears began to fall. "You remember how he would just show up. That nigga would come out of nowhere. I knew his ass was behind that damn chirping noise I would hear. I can't believe he drove that car out there. That's why the neighbors thought I came back. They saw my car but didn't see me."

Luther let Angel know he was going outside to smoke. He told Brooklin he loved her and to call the house later. He went on out the door and waited for Angel to come out.

Angel and Brooklin reminisced on all the times Vincent was popping up. Angel made the statement he probably killed Earl's brother just so he could have him to himself. Angel let Brooklin know that all that shit was going into her book.

Chapter 28

Do You

Reggie had gotten his out date. He was about to leave the level five camp and move to a level two. He had eight months to walk down.

He had his goons all in place. Two days before he was supposed to leave, Vincent arrived. He shot the breeze with him. Vincent told him he was there because the police traced C-Note's murder back to him. Reggie knew he was lying.

He guessed Vincent thought if he knew he had put some work in on Note that would save his ass. When Vincent walked towards the stall to take his leak, three of Reggie's goons got up on Vincent. He pissed his pants as he was repeatedly stabbed. Vincent didn't live one day behind the walls.

Ray was at the gym working out as usual. One of his old workers from off Beam Street walked up to him.

"LA Ray, what you been up to nigga?" said a buff caramel complexion man, drenched with sweat.

Ray looked at him. "Carlos?"

"Yeah nigga this me!"

"What you doing in my gym?"

"Man I just got home yesterday. My gal is swole

as a motha fucka. I bought her fat ass here to lose some weight. That shit is not healthy. I don't care how she look. I just want her to be healthy. I ain't 'bout to try to trust another bitch. I'm gone work with what I got."

"I hear that." Ray was trying to figure out what was he doing home. He got sentenced to twelve years FED time.

"Nigga you still moving weight?"

"Naw, Los man I don't fuck around." Ray shook his head and waved his hands.

"Ah you know that nigga Earl that used to be the man back in the day? All his brothers got killed and niggas went in there and took all they work." Carlos was trying to refresh Ray's memory.

"Yeah, I think I do remember that shit. That dude stay down the street from my kids."

"Yeah him. Do he still get it popping?" Carlos eyes were twinkling.

"Man, I don't know shit about that. I do me and I let them niggas in the street do them."

"Yeah, I'mma swing by his liquor store and see what's up. I gotta get my paper up. It's hard trying to make ends meet. Just coming home and nobody trying to give a job. I gotta get how I live."

"Do you nigga!" Ray walked away from Los. He realized how that boy had gotten home. He was running his mouth to damn much. "That's how he got locked up in the first damn place, running his mother fucking mouth."

Angel walked into the house and picked up the mail. She was surprised to see a letter from Mac Dre. He hadn't written Brooklin in years.

Dear Brooklin,

~ 162 ~

What's up witcha Boo. I know it's been a long time. I am sorry to hear about your mother. I was trying to send you and your family a sympathy card but I didn't have any money on my books. I got a lil' bullshit ass job in this joint. It only pays two dollars a day.

How are your boys? I know they probably real big by now. You got any more kids. I am quite sure you do. I know a nigga got with you fine ass and just want you to have his baby. I was trying to go half on a baby with yo ass myself.

I'm going to get straight to the point. You know

I'm up her with your sister's baby daddy, Reggie right.

That niggas a beast. He got this mother fucker on lock. He 'bout to come home though. He in another dorm.   He probably gone to another camp by now.

But check it. Some dudes took care of Vincent. Yeah the nigga is dead. He died his first day here. Shit happens like that here. Ain't nobody saying who did it.

That lil' shit was swept under the rug. The nigga had that coming. I was gone get his ass myself.

Well take care and get back at me. I still got love for you.

Love,
Mac Dre

"Nigga you still stupid. How you gone write in a letter you was going to get somebody. Angel balled the letter up and put it in the trash can. Brooklin didn't need to see that shit. Angel's cell phone began to ring. She pulled it from the clip that was on her waist. Looking at the caller ID on the screen, she knew who it was.

"Hey Teresa girl."

"What are you doing, Angel?"

"Nothing. Just walked in the door. I just made it back from David's Bridal. Kevin is going to send out letters to invite people to dinner so he could give them a formal letter as he asks them to participate in the wedding."

"Well, I was trying to see if you wanted to go to Jersey with me."

"We not taking any men with us." Angel wanted to know if Teresa's guy was going along. She didn't mind Kevin going but she was trying to be free from the people that she spent so much time with. She honestly needed some type to think.

"Naw it's just us girls." Teresa waved her hand in the air as if Angel could see her.

Ray was on his way to pick up Luther, the twins and Lil Reggie to take them to school. They were having donuts for dads at the school. Kevin wanted to attend but it was taking place on a Tuesday and that was one of the days he had to work.

Ray saw Passion going into the Royal Palace on Natural Bridge. He was wondering why she would be entering a lounge so early in the morning and why was she there on a weekday. To put out the spark to his curiosity, he pulled onto the lot to follow.

Ray walked in the RP and she was standing over at the window to order some food. He knew the RP had that fire when it came to breakfast and shrimp. Passion walked away from the counter and sat at the table near the dance floor. She had the Evening Whirl, a local newspaper with the grimiest news, in front of her so she didn't see him approaching.

"Hey miss lady," Ray smiled.

"What you up to, stranger?" Passion called him a stranger because when he saw he wasn't getting the goods, his phone calls stopped. She laid the newspaper down on the table.

Ray looked down at the paper. Something stuck out like as sore thumb and grabbed his attention. Earl McClendon's picture was blasted on the front page. He was being indicted cn drug charges. Ray shook his head. It was approximately a week ago that he bumped into Carlos in the gym and he had mentioned his name.

"I see you strolling up in here and I was curious what brought you over here on the north side of St. Louis."

Passion looked up to Ray as her date was entering the RP. She waved him in her direction. "A friend of mine told me that the Royal Palace had some FYRE ass breakfast."

"Hey what's up, Ray!" Carlos reached to give him some daps.

Ray looked him over, "Man snitches get stitches." He turned to Passion, "Do you Ma!"

Ray laughed as he walked out the place. It was no coincidence that Carlos was in the gym that day. He didn't know why it wasn't him on the front page of the paper but he was sure enough glad he wasn't. He thanked God as he got back in his car.

Ray had made it to pick up Luther and the boys. They made it to school a little late but the event hadn't taken place just yet.

Tables were set up in the school's gymnasium. There was an array of donuts to choose from. Ray followed Luther as he walked to the front of the gym near a corner. Their table happened to be near the only nearest exit besides the door they had entered. Luther sat facing the door. Ray noticed that he did the same thing when they went to the Pink Slip.

"Luther, why do you always sit near exits and shit?" Ray pulled his chair out to sit down.

"You mean to tell me that as long as you been in the game, you never placed yourself where you can see everybody coming and going in a spot you can leave out quickly if anything pops off!" Luther winked his eye.

"You know one thing, I ain't never had myself out there like that. Motha fuckas don't even know me. That's just how I like it."

Kevin dropped Angel and Teresa off at Lambert Airport. They made it to Newark International Airport. The girls exited the airport and crossed the street to stand in line for a taxi.

Once in the taxi, they rode through the city. The taxi driver was giving them their own personal tour. When they arrived at the Ramada Inn, Teresa paid the fare and Angel tipped the driver.

Angel went into their hotel room. She hit the bed and was knocked out by the time Teresa came out of the restroom. Teresa woke her up. "Girl, you didn't come here to sleep!"

"I thought we weren't going anywhere until Saturday." Angel literally dragged her body to the restroom.

They walked out of the hotel and into a taxi that took them from the Jersey turnpike and through the Holland tunnel.

Angel looked around. "I should have brought my father with me. He's from Brooklyn."

"So that's why your sister and brother have those names. When we were in school, I used to wonder why they were named that." Teresa laughed.

"He doesn't talk much about it. When we were young, he would tell us when it comes to one project to another, they were all the same." Angel laughed thinking about her younger days.

Teresa and Angel took pictures in front of The Apollo. Ending up in Times Square, they grabbed a bite to eat at Sbarro's. Times Square to SoHo. SoHo is a neighborhood in lower Manhattan. Teresa went Gucci, Louie Vuitton, and Coco Chanel crazy!

"Angel, girl you don't wanna none of this stuff."
"Naw Teresa, do you and knock yourself out." Angel waved her hand.

"You can take this shit back to the Lou and sell this shit." Teresa grabbed a plentiful amount of purses, sunglasses, and watches.

Once they made it back to the hotel, Angel lay

down and lost herself in her thoughts. She knew that walking away or ignoring the situation wasn't the best way to come to a resolution in solving the dilemma; only she knew what she was dealing with. The day she met Kevin at the gas station, she believed he was her blessing in disguise but she was coming to a conclusion of letting the chips fall where they may lay.

Angel had been creating a sense of mystery about her and Kevin's relationship. It all heightened Kevin's desires to get to know her even more.

Kevin would try to convince her about the way things should be between them throughout the years. That meant marriage to him. He had grown concerned for the betterment of Angel and Lil Reggie. That was the core reason why Angel appreciated him. It was not time for her to let go and move on.

Her past relationship and the history with Reggie burdened her. She couldn't see a broader vision from holding on to the past even after all the years she and Kevin shared. The gesture he made with the car was a first. He bought small things for birthdays and holidays. She knew that he wasn't trying to buy her love. She was going to focus on the big picture and relax while she was on the East Coast.

Chapter 29

YOU AND ME

Brooklin walked around the corner to Tolliver's liquor store. She hadn't been around there in years. She would have driven but she was trying to clear her mind and enjoy the fresh air. Had she had somewhere else to go, she would have gone somewhere. She just settled on the local store.

When she made it to the store, Boogey was right in front as usual.

"Hey Pepa, where's Salt? I can't do my dance all low and stuff." Boogey showed his toothless smile.

"Boogey, I don't know why you can't do your dance alone now. You been doing it for years by yo damn self." Brooklin walked into the store. She came back out with her items in a brown paper bag.

"How have you been doing? I know you just got home. So sorry to hear about yawl's loss." You could see the sincerity in his eyes.

"I'm out the motha fucking Workhouse and I'm free!" Brooklin laughed.

"That's the damn Jerk house. They be jerking motha fuckas around." Boogey thought about his days being locked up at the Medium Security facility.

"I know what you saying. It is what it is, but I miss momma though." Brooklin walked away with her head hung low.

Boogey shouting "Keep ya head up!" was drowned out by the passing cars.

Brooklin made it back home. She decided to continue to stay outside for a while. The spring breezes were settling. Brooklin reached into her bag and pulled out one of her bags of chips. She opened her bag of Red Hot Riplets and twisted the cap off her Mountain Dew. With her head leaned back, she began to take a swig of her soda, noticing a midnight blue Jaguar pulling up.

She watched Joe-Joe as he parked. When he pulled onto the street, he saw Brooklin as she sat outside. He walked over to her porch.

He was dressed in his olive green uniform with a plentiful amount of badges, medals, and stars. Joe-Joe was the youngest black Four Star General in the Air Force.

Brooklin stood to embrace him. Then she plastered a wet kiss on his cheek and he, in return, kissed her forehead.

Brooklin leaned back, "Damn nigga the Air Force got you pushing a Jag. Get back let me check you out." She leaned back as he smiled. Joe-Joe was no longer that puny four-eyed first love. He had a body like Vin Diesel and a face like Dominique Wilkins when he played for the Atlanta Hawks back in the day.

Joe-Joe sat down on the porch. Brooklin grabbed her seat next to him.

"I'm sorry about Auntie. I know that was the closest thing y'all had to a mother. Sorry I didn't make it to the funeral. I am quite sure you know I was locked up in the Workhouse getting jerked around."

"Yeah. That whole ordeal was shitty. Why they keep you so long?" Joe-Joe shook his head sideways.

"They were bullshitting. Steady continuing my case and shit. Then the damn public pretender quit and moved to Barbados."

"That's why motherfuckers be calling the Workhouse the Jerk house. Then the damn public defenders don't be doing shit. Man, if you ain't got the money, crime don't pay. Mess around and be jammed up real quick." Joe-Joe

"That is so true." Brooklin nodded in agreement with him.

They sat quietly for a moment and just watched the traffic go by. A new couple was moving into where Mr. Whitey stayed. It appeared to be a young married couple with two small children.

"I wish we could just go back to when we were kids. Remember when Tim, Terrell, and Chad's dad would cut that damn porch light on and they would wait a few minutes before they went in the house."

Joe-Joe laughed, "They used to play it off going in the house one-by-one. Like we didn't know what was going on. Had they been outside a tad bit longer, they would have known our asses had to go in shortly after them."

"You shole right. We knew when they went in our time was slowly approaching." Brooklin chuckled.

Another quiet moment fell upon them. Brooklin drank her soda and ate some more of her chips. She offered Joe-Joe some. He grabbed the bag and dumped a few chips into his hand.

"What happen to Vincent?" Joe-Joe wasn't the one to beat around the bush. He wanted to know what he was charged with and any other information she offered.

"You know I can't bring myself to understand why he did that. Angel told me that my momma had a brain aneurysm, but do you know he hit her several times. I play our conversations over in my head when we did eventually start to spend time together." Brooklin paused and Joe-Joe sat attentively listening.

"I told that boy that I felt like my momma was the only one that really cared about me and he took that from me. I actually think that he thought him taking her away from me that he would be the only one left that truly cared about me."

Joe-Joe looked her in her eyes, "That nigga is crazy."

"He was crazy. That nigga got knocked as soon as he stepped foot in the penitentiary. I don't know who did it. I am just glad they did it. Then some days I wish he could have sat and rot to death. I be thinking as if he had an easy way out. I feel like I was the one that lost out in the long run. Feel what I'm saying?" Brooklin turned and looked at Joe-Joe as if she had something serious to say, "I think this family is cursed with tragedy. My grandmother was murdered and my father's mother died giving birth to him."

"I wouldn't say it's a curse. One thing, we all got to do is die. Ain't no running from that. Believe it or not that's one appointment you are not going to miss." Joe-Joe tried to keep his composure looking at her with a serious supportive look. "How is Harlem doing?"

"You know that nigga married him a white chick. He don't fuck with us. He hangs around about a bunch of damn white people. I ain't saying he wrong, but damn we family. My daddy used to tell us that blood is thicker than water. Harlem just done shitted on us! Ya hear me!"

"I wouldn't say that. Maybe that's just the way he is dealing with his problems. Only looking forward and not looking back."

"He really changed. He used to look out for us though. Harlem really looked out for Angel. I think they still talk every now and then. She used to be straight scared of his ass. Did you know she was scared to tell him she was pregnant? I think if Harlem was still here Double R probably wouldn't never gotten to tap that ass!"

"Naw she gave it up. She was gone give it to him cause she wanted that nigga to have that!" Joe-Joe said so serious.
They both laughed.

"We sitting up here talking about me and my crazy ass family, what you been up to."

"It time for me to re-enlist. I don't know what I want to do."

"What do you do in the Air Force?"

"I'm a pilot."

"Where were you when that nine-eleven shit happened?"

"I was in Italy. Being that I have a high ranking, I am the last on the totem pole to go."

Kevin and Angel pulled up in front of the house. They sat in the car looking up on the porch. Angel told Kevin about how she was disgusted with Brooklin when she kissed Joe-Joe during a game of Truth or Dare.
Kevin rolled down his window, "Do you two little lovebirds wanna go get something to eat?"

Joe-Joe looked at Brooklin as he whispered, "Play along with me." He gave Brooklin a long passionate kiss. He had been longing for that moment. He wasn't ready to stop when Brooklin let go.

Brooklin playfully slapped his shoulder. They got up and walked up to Kevin's truck. Joe-Joe opened the door for Brooklin and walked around to the other side. Joe-Joe and Kevin were introduced and they headed towards their destination.

Chapter 30

HONEY I'M HOME

"What's going on, Double R?" Midnight grabbed his friend, pulled him towards him and patted him on his back. "You swole as motha fucka! What you bench press? Three fifty?"

"Get yo black ass on," Reggie snickered. "I heard you caught a lil' case."

"Man, that's a bunch of bullshit. I got pulled over with a blunt in my ashtray. You know that punk ass officer locked me up. He didn't even search the car. I got served with a year on papers. Now I gotta go piss once a month," Midnight sneered.

"What else been up?"

"Peep and Cent Dog wanna take you out. I told them you were coming home." Midnight looked at Reggie.

"Man, I ain't trying to go out. I dun seen niggas for twelve years of my life every motha fucking day. I'mma go out but not right now. A nigga trying to knock the lining out some shit." Reggie grabbed his crotch.

"Yo ass ain't had no pussy in twelve years?! That's fucked up!"

"Nigga don't get it twisted. I was fucking this nurse in the infirmary and this CO. Shit, I hit Tawanna a couple times in the visiting room. I walked these last eight months down with no pussy. They moved me to a lower level. You know I was brand new there. I wasn't focusing on shit but coming home."

"How the fuck you hit that girl in the visiting room?" Midnight poked his lips out in disbelief.

"She would get there early with four of her partners. See, I was hooking motha fuckas up with her friends. See in the morning, only one CO was working the visiting room. Another one wouldn't come 'til an hour or two later. Check it. The CO would sit in the back of the room. They didn't have a straight look over on the left side of the room where the vending machine and microwave was. We would stand right up under the security mirror that faced the microwave. The four other couples stood around us like they were warming up something or looking to purchase something out the vending machine."

"You mean to tell me they stood there and watched."

"Yeah nigga. We took turns doing that shit. We was smooth with it. If they were paying attention, they would have known whichever bitch wore a skirt out of the bunch, she was the motha fucka getting hit!"

Midnight shook his head as Reggie laughed.

"You talked to Angel?"

"Man, I don't know if I even wanna talk to her. It's like I couldn't control shit she was doing while I was inside. Now that I'm free, I don't think I could deal with her rejection. She probably doesn't love me, but I never stop loving her. Angel is the only girl I ever loved. I only been with two girls and Tawanna wasn't shit."

"Man, that's why you need to go out and meet some new pussy."

"I ain't trying fuck around like that. Nigga, I avoided death from the streets. I ain't trying to let a piece of ass kill me." Reggie looked Midnight over.

"Nigga, quit making excuses. Yo ass don't wanna go out 'cause that ass scared." Midnight let out a few chuckles.

"Hello Mr. St. James could you let Lil Reggie know that I am on my way." Angel listened for his answer and closed her cell phone.

Reggie and Midnight stood watching the burgundy BMW as it parked.

"Who is that?" Reggie continued to watch.

"That's yo BMW." Midnight walked to the top of the steps so he could have a better view.

"My what!" Reggie watched the car door open.

Angel got out of the car. This was the first

time he had seen her without a ponytail. She was wearing a Jacquelyn Smith from Charlie's Angel look.

She hadn't noticed Reggie standing three houses down from his house at Midnight's house.

"Angel!" He began to walk towards her.

She wanted to run towards him. Then she had thoughts of getting back in her car. Stopping in her tracks, she looked him over. Here they were all grown up and she was getting butterflies. A sense of guilt fell upon her as childhood memories started to override her guilt. As he got closer, she thought about Run DMC because he was looking just like Jam Master Jay. She wanted to bust a rap and let him finish the line. Sporting a white linen pantsuit with a linen cami and gold high heel BCBG's, she was feeling too classy.

"Easily I approach…" Reggie reached out.

"The microphone cuz I ain't no joke." Angel caught and finalized the hold. They held each other for a while. She closed her eyes and inhaled his scent.

"You looking good," she smiled.

"You're riding good," Reggie said as he looked at the car.

Angel didn't want to turn around. The car was not a subject she was trying to touch. That meant talking about Kevin. She wasn't ready to address that subject. There was no reason for this feeling; she just felt she owed him an explanation.

"Nobody told me you were home. My own son hadn't

called me to tell me."

"We hung out all weekend," Reggie grinned.

"When you get home?"

"I came home Thursday. I went with my daddy when he went and picked him up from school. I wanted to take him to the barber with me, but he wants Kevin to cut his hair."

Hearing Kevin's name made the butterflies return. Mixed emotions were running wild and the truth is she was overreacting. Reggie was still in love with her, but him being the standup dude that he was, he was able to cope and deal with the situation.

Reality had set in with Angel. She didn't think she couldn't overcome her feelings and Kevin would be the one that got hurt. She had been shopping for wedding stuff all weekend long. She had gotten everything she needed. They had not set a date yet. That was only because she was tormenting herself, but Kevin told her he was ready when she was.

She wanted to tell Reggie all of the new things that were taking place with her like school and her car. Those things involved Kevin so she decided against it. The subject of choice was their son. She talked about how good he was in school and how much he had grown.

Reggie let her know that he went to the classroom to meet his teacher and the teacher asked if he was his uncle that moved to Alabama and became a lawyer. She even added that she met his father and his grandfather; and it was a good thing that he had so many positive role models in his life. He finished by saying that he didn't want to tell her he was his daddy fresh out the penitentiary.

Angel stood there listening. That's when she realized no conversation was safe with Reggie. Kevin became a constant part of both her and her son's life.

Reggie got in the car with Midnight. He had him take him to Tawanna's house. When he knocked on the door, he could hear her yelling from the back of the house. The television was drowning him saying "Reggie."

She snatched the door open. Reggie and Midnight stood looking at the people that sat right by the door watching TV. Trash was scattered throughout the house. Tawanna knew it was foul because she stood in the doorway not trying to let him in.

She wasn't offering and he damn sure was not about to ask.

"Why the fuck you ain't call nobody and tell them you were coming home?" Tawanna was demanding an answer. All the while she came to see him, she had her hair done. Today, it was all over her head. She was looking like the hood rat she was.

Reggie had no answer. He had a question that he was burning to ask. He wanted to know why her house was so nasty. Furthermore, who was the grown ass motha fuckas that were sitting in that nasty shit?

"Man, I'mma wait in the car." Midnight walked back to the car. When he got in the car, he rambled through his CDs. He was looking for a song he needed to play. It was killing him that he couldn't find the CD. He was looking for "Nasty Bitch," but he couldn't find it. His eighty-eight Oldsmobile began to blast the sounds of Project Pat featuring Ludacris and Crunchy Black's *Dis Bitch Dat Hoe*.

Reggie stood there nodding his head to the beat smiling. Tawanna pulled the door up and sat down.

Reggie sat down beside her.

"You know I drove up there to see you Saturday?" Tawanna looked him over.

He sat there thinking about fucking. He liked Tawanna but he didn't know if those feelings were there because she risked her life for him or because she filled a void. What he did know was that he wanted to get up inside some hot pussy. Angel and Tawanna were his only two choices. He doubted that he had a chance with Angel so he was settling for option number two. He had his dose of serenity. Now he needed to release. For the last eight months, Rosie Palm and her five sisters was the only thing he was getting up with. The whole time Tawanna talked, he was thinking of what was of importance to him. When she asked what he was doing later on, the light bulb over his head came on.

"I'm trying to see you, but I know you don't want me to come back over here." He didn't want to go in there but he was ready to make things happen and he didn't care about trash or kids.

"I can come get you and we can go get a room."

"What time?" Reggie grinned.

"Now! It's up to you."

"I'll give you time to clean up. I mean get yourself together and when I think you ready, I'll call you."

Reggie walked off the porch and got in the car. "You wrong for playing that song."

"I was trying to find something else." Midnight looked at Reggie.

"That was one for me. Cuz, I'm trying to see that pussy hole soaking fucking wet." Reggie laughed, "Take me to get some condoms cause I be damned if I am running up in that raw!"

"Didn't you hit raw when you was locked up?" Midnight asked sarcastically.

"Fuck you nigga!" Reggie laughed, knowing his friend was speaking some facts.

Chapter 31

MISS ME WITH THAT FOOLISHNESS

"Angel, tell me why Brooklin is picking Reggie up from his grandparents. You didn't have a problem with me picking him up previously. Mr. St. James doesn't have a problem with it. So tell me what your problem is with it?" Kevin waited patiently for her to respond. He had noticed lately there had been a change in her behavior. It now seemed as if she was trying to keep him a secret.

He continued to look at her as she searched through her thoughts in finding an explanation. Taking a deep breath, she spoke. "Kevin, Reggie is at home."

"Okay, why haven't you introduced us?" Kevin wanted to know why his fiancée was concerned about where her ex was.

With a swing of the neck and a spin of the eye, she said, "He don't wanna meet you."

With much confidence as always, he chose his words carefully. "Look here, if I were him, I would want to meet me. I would need to know the man who has been active and supportive in my child's life."

"You two are so different. You would never understand." Angel didn't know how Reggie felt. She just felt the urge to protect his feelings.

"What the fuck is that supposed to mean? What? 'Cause I ain't never done a motherfucking drive-by I am different? I grew up on the North Side of St. Louis. That part of the city breeds nothing but thoroughbred ass niggas. So I guess you think I am an ole soft ass nigga. Angel, you don't even know me!" Kevin felt the need to let her know where he stood.

Angel felt as if she didn't know him. In all those years, she had never heard him curse. This was a little strange to her. He was starting to sound like a stand up dude. When she first met him, he appeared to have that T.I. "Grand Hustle" demeanor. He never showed it until today. Thoughts ran wild because she actually thought that Kevin didn't want to see Reggie. At this very moment, she knew he was very capable of holding his own. She never thought of him as being soft, but she never thought he would go hard. Angel actually underestimated him. She just knew he was nothing like Reggie.

Kevin walked over in front of Angel and looked down into her eyes as she stood by the dresser.

"Angel, for a long time I have been in love with you. I want you to know that I would never do anything stupid to leave y'all alone. With me by your side, you will never have to worry about a sleepless night. I want to grow old with you. Lil Reggie and you both have softened my heart," he paused.

"After I lost my parents, I have worked to prevent everyone else from going through what I went through. I stopped caring about my own happiness. I did what I did to make me happy. My happiness wasn't obtained until I found you. Believe it or not, the day I met you at the gas station, I said that you were going to be my wife."

Angel looked at him with tears in her eyes as he continued. "This whole ordeal is making me light hearted. All due to the fact, the seriousness of my love for you encourages me to bring nothing but pleasurable moments into your life. We can experience happiness together without having to justify it to anybody including Reggie. Don't be afraid to let go of the past and grab all of your impulsive desires. Be real with me and yourself. That's all I'm asking right now."

Kevin placed his hands on her shoulders. "I shared your grief of sorrow just as much as you did. You didn't know how bad I wanted to take over your pain so that you didn't have to bear any. You know why I did it that? I did and I do everything because I love you! Do you know what love means or do you even care? I guess this is just my dilemma."

Kevin walked away before Angel could get a glimpse of his tears. Angel had it bad, but the words touched her heart. She knew she still had a place in Reggie's heart. Things seemed so much different when he was not able to be seen daily. But now that he was present, she just wanted some closure.

She wanted to call him back and tell him she was sorry but she didn't know what she was apologizing for. Angel was at a loss for words and caught up in some foolish emotions. She realized one thing.

Chapter 32

IT AIN'T NO FUN IF THE HOMIES CAN'T HAVE NONE

Brooklin pulled up in front of Reggie's house. She stepped out of her car so that she could knock on the door. She had a problem with people blowing. When they stayed in the projects and the fellas would blow, the hot tail girls, whom Luther named them, would go running to the blow. She could remember Luther saying "Hoes go to blows" in the back of her mind.

As she walked up to the door, Peep Dog was coming out of Reggie's house. "Hey, Brooklin, how have you been doing? You looking good as a motha fucka." Peep hollered back in the door, "Hey R, Brooklin out here, wit her fine ass."

Keena came to the door. She stood there and looked at Brooklin. "Do you know who I am?"

Brooklin looked at this young thick teenage girl. Wearing professionally done micro-braids and diamond studded earrings, this young girl looked like new money. The thickness of her thighs gripped the Nike Air nylon green shorts tightly.

Keena's white on white hi-tops/Air Forces were flawless matching her green and white Nike Air T-shirt. Brooklyn's thoughts were like "Do I suppose to know who the fuck you are? I hope you are not about to tell me you are Lil Reggie's girlfriend or Reggie's daughter." She stood there thinking of something to say and Keena just smiled.

"I don't believe you don't know me. I used to come over your house when I was little." Keena smiled.

Peep Dog sat back observing Brooklin. "That's Scary's daughter."

"Damn you have gotten big!" Brooklin gave her a hug. "If Angel sees you, I betcha she won't know who you are. What grade are you in?"

"I am in the eighth-grade," Keena smiled.

"It has been a long time. Do you have our number?" Brooklin asked.

Keena nodded, "Lil Reggie gave it to me."

Peep Dog reached out to touch Brooklin in the mid-section of her back. "I don't have your number."

She smiled, "You didn't ask me for it either."

Brooklin and Peep Dog exchanged numbers. He walked off and got in his car. Brooklin watched as he got in his black Dodge Charger. "Rimmed up and tinted up just how I like it." Brooklin said to herself. She and Lil Reggie headed to her car.

Brooklin went by Ray's to get her boys. She was taking them out to Dave and Buster's. Ray was upset that he had to give her money to go when she was taking them. He wanted to go along but he didn't feel like getting brushed off by Brooklin.

Since she had been home, he wanted to talk to her. He wanted to let her know that he still cared. He thought he had to be insane for never letting go. She was the mother of his children. Ray just merely thought about her walking out on him claiming females were playing on the phone. He knew this wasn't possible because he never gave his home number out. But two things tied them together.

Ray felt that Brooklin was so exciting to be around. She was more than a lover. She was his friend and the mother of his children. He thought they shared something special, but Brooklin thought otherwise. Her biggest fear was Ray doing what Luther did her mother.

Finally, at Dave and Buster's, Brooklin bought the power cards, went, and ordered herself some hot wings and a Bud Light. The boys were so busy driving on the *Fast and Furious* driving game and playing skee-ball so intensely that they didn't want to eat. She didn't bother them. She figured she would get them something on the way home.

Brooklin made it home and found Luther in his bedroom watching television. She got up in the bed with him. He was watching *The Wire*. She tried to talk to him but he concentrated on the program. Trying to go to sleep, things became complicated. Brooklin left her father so that he could continue watching his favorite program.

Brooklin hopped into the shower. When she reached her room, the phone was ringing. She answered hearing Peep Dog's voice. He was now under investigation. Wanting to know his government name and where he stayed, she started scrutinizing him.

Walking outside to get inside his Charger, she now knew she was going with Darrell Blackman. Darrell paid attention to everything going on. He had pretty much been on point at all times. He was working at the local boys and girls club as an athletic director.

Peep Dog and Brooklin cruised throughout the city. Doing nothing but burning a bunch of gas. He watched Brooklin as she smoked three blunts. He got on Highway 270 and headed towards Natural Bridge Road. Pulling up at the Holiday Inn, Peep got out of the car and paid for the room. After he squared the room away, he went to the gas station down the street to grab him some condoms.

Back in the room, they both felt each other up. Brooklin moved in slow motion as she gave him a strip tease. He smiled, checking out her feminine muscular frame. His manhood stood at attention. He had admired Brooklin back in high school. She never said two words to him. Right now, he was happier than a punk in the penitentiary.

Brooklin stopped the slow grinding. "Now you brought me here and didn't ask me did I wanna come. I'm just going to assume you wanna smell my poo-nanny. Well, just so you will know, blunts can't pay for this and I don't give away free pussy." Brooklin pointed to her crotch. "This shit right here bought me a Benz."

"I gotta buy you a damn car for that shit?" He chuckled.

"You ain't gotta buy no damn car, but just so you'll know, niggas in the Lou are willing to pay top dollar for this."

"That shit got frequent flyer miles. Shit, can a nigga get a friends and family discount?" Peep looked at Brooklin serious than a heart attack.

"You got jokes. Now peep this, Peep Dog. Since you dun spent yo money, you can give me some head, but if you wanna go further than that you got to come up off some change. Best believe you gone lick it before you stick it."

He sat on the edge of the bed flicking through the channels. What he wanted to do was slap the shit out of her. Rationalizing the whole situation, he believed she was right. He brought her there against her will, but when she crossed that threshold, it was fair game.

Brooklin looked at him horny, as a motherfucker. This was a first. It worked on Mac Dre and Eric. She noticed that he was working with something 'cause his pole was trying to burst out of his sweats. He was sitting there hard as a rock and was more interested in what was going on the television while he flicked through the channels.

He could see her out of the corner of his eye. Since she was undressed, he pulled her towards him. Brooklin was literally putting it in his face.

She was creaming as he slowly liked her insides. Brooklin grabbed the top of his bald head guiding him with her movements as she rocked her hips. It was all good at first. When he noticed she was about to reach that peak, he stopped. He was expecting her to flip the fuck out. She lay down beside him and wasn't afraid to touch herself. She got herself off and fell asleep.

He couldn't believe he was the one that came up short. He wasn't anticipating on that happening. His attentions were to get her wide open and have her begging for some of his beef.

Peep attempted to make his move. Advancing on her unconsciousness, he had every intention on knocking her down. As he made her love come down, she perked up and became quickly aroused. Going ten rounds without any rest, Brooklin was wondering what type of drugs he was on. She bounced and twirled, shaking her hips from the left to the right. Her pussy was so sore and wore out, she had to massage him to get him off on that last round.

Brooklin played that role in the beginning trying not to give it up for free. He sucked on her melons and ate the shit out of her peach. Ass was jiggling and smacking. He pulled her back several times as she was trying to service him some head. He let her know if she wasn't swallowing there was no need to waste her time. She did it like a pro. He damn near was in love with little Miss Brooklin.

They kicked it for a minute. Then all of a sudden she stopped calling him.

Reggie rolled up to The Broadway with Midnight, Peep and Cent-Dog. Reggie was flossing his Dodge Charger on twenty-two inch Giovanna rims looking like his was on a quest to be rich. Peep Dog rolled his Charger with its factory rims. He had given his previous rims to Reggie. He was waiting on the new rims he ordered to come in.

Double R was back. His diamonds blinged and haters couldn't stop his shine. Reggie and his crew walked into the club looking like new money. The haters mean mugged.

Peep Dog saw Brooklin on the dance floor, grinding as if somebody was hitting her from the back. The Broadway was crunk. There were more people in the club than it allowed. DJ AJ was bringing the heater through the speakers.

They made their way to the VIP section at the

top of the club. Overlooking everything that was going on, Reggie was able to keep an eye on Angel. She had style and finesse as he noticed her in her Prada sport denim jean with a black Prada Luna Rossa fitted tee. Her hair was pulled back in a ponytail as he remembered. It just moved from the side to smack dead in center of her head.

2Pac's *How Long Will They Mourn Me* played over the beat of MC Breed's and 2Pac's *Gotta Get Mine* followed by Master P featuring Silkk the Shocker and Pimp C's *I Miss My Homies*. He finished the mix with the Dirty Rotten Scoundrels' *Gangsta Lean* over Luniz's *I Got Five On It* beat.

The DJ had Reggie and his boys in a zone. They all were reminiscing about their lost homeboys. Peep Dog snapped out of the zone when he saw Carlos walking towards him.

Carlos knew all the boys from grade school. His mother moved before that static kicked off. She moved over on Beam Street so therefore his gang of choice was the Bloods. Tonight, no one was on any gang shit. They were enjoying themselves. Carlos waved his hand towards Reggie, "Come here derrty let me holla at you."

Reggie waved his hand in midair. "I ain't fucking with you Los. Niggas trying to see that your toe is tagged."

"Keep it moving. Nigga ain't nobody fucking wit yo hot ass." Midnight mean mugged him.

Reggie decided to move closer to the dance floor so that Angel could see him. He hadn't realized Angel saw him as he walked in. Like he watched her, she was watching him. When Alicia Keys and Usher were talking about *My Boo*, that song fit them perfectly and it all started when they were at a very young age.

With his friends following, Reggie headed

toward the direction in which he saw Angel sitting, at a table towards the front of the club. Everyone had adequate space to get comfortable because the dance floor was packed with people doing their own form of two stepping.

Whispering in her ear, he said, "What you drinking?"

Keeping her composure, she replied, "Grey Goose and cranberry."

"A lot has changed since I've been gone." Reggie waved to get the attention of the waitress.

Midnight grabbed Brooklin's hand and led her to the dance floor. Peep Dog watched as Brooklin gyrated all over Midnight. He was trying not to trip off the fact she just up and stopped calling him. As other women moved through the club, he reached out grabbing at them until someone finally stopped and had a conversation with him. He was overdoing it. Keeping one eye on Brooklin and the other on the chic that was exposing damn near all of her breasts, he made conversation. The music was too loud. The female was just acting like she could hear him.

When Avant featuring Wyatt's *My First Love* began to play, Reggie grabbed Angel's hand to pull her up from the table. Standing near where they sat, he slow danced singing the sweet sounds of the song in her ear. She rested her head on his shoulder. His touch was delicate as she remembered.

Peep Dog leaned in, talking to the both of them. "That's what the dance floor is for."

They both looked at him laughing. As the song was coming to an end, Angel reached for her seat. All that changed when DJ AJ came back with Keke Wyatt's *Nothing In This World*.

Angel led Reggie to the center of the dance floor. She sang the whole song to him. Angel looked him directly in his eyes as she told him it was all about him. He listened as if she was talking to him and thinking the song was coming straight from her heart.

Ginuwine's *My Pony* came through the song as it ended. Reggie sang it with a smile letting Angel know his saddle was ready for her to jump on it. He playfully grabbed the back of her ponytail as she walked away. Kevin had seen enough. He turned to exit the club.

Last call for alcohol was announced. Midnight wanted to know was Angel going to leave with Reggie. Reggie shrugged his shoulders letting him know that he didn't have a clue to what type of arrangements she was making. He would have desired her to go. All the dancing had him ready to feel her insides, but he could just settle for that little time they had shared. Tawanna's fucking was good enough for him. She just wasn't that special one that made his life complete.

Brooklin and Midnight had other plans. Midnight was ready for Reggie to take him to his car. Somehow Brooklin manipulated Angel to follow them to the Motel 6 not too far from the club.

Chapter 33

CONGRATULATIONS

Brooklin sat in the car while Midnight went to go meet with his probation officer. They had had a long night and he didn't have time to drop her off.

She sat in the car watching this dude walking back and forth like he was anxiously waiting on someone. As she turned up the radio, she laughed thinking about the escapade she had last night. Midnight came up short. His dick was lost in the darkness, but his mouth was like a hurricane.

Brooklin watched and noticed that the anxious fella was a familiar face. She was trying to think why C-Note called him Flintstone when he was short like Barney Rubble. She figured when Flintstone walked back towards the car, she would get out and speak to him. He didn't look like the Flintstone she remembered. She blamed it on the drugs. He had never been the same since C-Note had been murdered.

Brooklin started to sing with the song on the radio.

"I don't wish you no bad luck…"

Shots rang out. She looked to the right of her and noticed Midnight had been shot. Brooklin sat frozen. A panic attack snuck right up on her. Tears rolled down her face while her mouth screamed uncontrollably. She rocked back and forth as she watched Flintstone run off making a dash for the corner. He disappeared just as quickly as Midnight's life had been brought to an end.

When the paramedics came, Brooklin was no help. She couldn't tell them what happened at all. As Midnight lay on the concrete, she had visions of her mother. The first responding officer looked through her purse. One witness was able to tell the police that Brooklin sat in the car as the assailant approached the victim. Brooklin was dropped off at home and Luther was instructed to give the officer a call when he felt as though she was ready to cooperate.

Reggie sat on the porch with his son. He was asking him what he wanted to be when he grew up. It hurt him to his heart to hear his child he wanted to be a firefighter just like Kevin. The wanting to be like Kevin didn't bother him. It was the fact that he hadn't done anything positive in his life that his son could be proud of. Since he had come home, he was trying to catch up with what he had lost. He would pick his son up from school every day. After he was done helping him with his homework, they would have dinner right before he took him home. Reggie cherished Fridays because he got to stay the weekend.

His devastation was interrupted as he watched the officers walk up on Midnight's porch. His mother came to the door and in seconds, she was screaming "Not my baby!" Reggie ran to see what the commotion was all about.

He lost his second brother.

Reggie had been breaking laws all of his life. He came home and everything was all good in his hood. He got in his car to ease some of his pain. Thoughts of wanting to talk to Angel tempted him to go by her house. He thought otherwise of it.

He drove and blazed up his blunt. Going a few blocks over, he saw that Midnight's goons were standing on the corner, posted like a lamppost still slanging rocks and throwing up gang signs. He shook his head in disgust. But he knew the little soldiers would need a new role model. He was going to make sure he would be there to lead the way. So many crews were set tripping. The crew he once had was slowly diminishing. The north side was filled with gorillas and real niggas who had ceased with the static. Over on the Horseshoe and Beam Street, niggas were still screaming and bringing drama to everybody. Accomac cats were still being buried. Everybody was trying to split somebody's wig.

He heard about more murders while being locked down. The thuggish nigga in him wanted to retaliate. Were these sets really ready to feel the wrath of a real menace? Back in the day, he wasn't taking no shorts or any losses and everybody that stood on the corner was a goner. He and his team made sure of that. He realized that he didn't have the team he once had so it was now time to do a little recruiting. Midnight had already had that in place. It was only right for him to step in. He made the little goons some offers that they couldn't refuse.

Reggie armed them with some artillery free of charge. He fronted them their work. He allowed them to get their paper. The young goons felt so good in their new outfits. Although they were living like peasants, they thought they were living like kings. But like in every crew, there has to be a stand up dude.

Toussaint was this yellow motha fucka with curly locks. Standing six feet tall, even with an athletic build, he didn't look like any average

sixteen-year-old. Reggie would get him all amped
when he would address him as T-Murder. Dude had never
murdered anyone, but his scandalous look showed
everyone that he had murdering potential. He was the
one that kept the goons in line when Midnight wasn't
around. Everybody else had the Pinky and The Brain
mentality. Toussaint was definitely The Brain.

The belly of the beast was the only thing
promised and death stood around the corner. Reggie
saw the penitentiary clearer in his future. It had
already taken too much time away from his son. He
looked to the skies and realized too many of his boys
were gone too soon. Had they put down the guns and
raised their fists, they could still be here to
reminisce. Still with his head toward the sky, he
thought aloud, "Midnight rest your soul and I will
see you when I get there." Knowing he would never let
go of his memories, he thought of his brother
Richard, Scary and Clack.

Midnight went and bought himself some blue
spray paint. Coming back home, he pulled into the
alley behind an abandoned building. He drew a mural
of all of his boys. The mural was titled, "This Is
for My Homies." He had rediscovered his hidden talent
while being locked down.

Angel ran into the house and just barely made
it to the restroom. Coming out the restroom, she
bumped into Luther.

"Angel, don't let a good thang go down the
drain. I can't tell you what to do, but I can tell
you that he loves you. If I don't know anything at
all, I do know true love when I see it. When you have
a feeling that you can't leave, that's love. It's
like the light when you can't see and the air when
you can't breathe. Those types of feelings are rare.

Besides, he has much more to offer you and my grandson."

Angel looked him in his eyes. "Daddy where's Brooklin?"

She went to her father's bedroom. Brooklin was curled up like a newborn his bed.

"Brooklin what's wrong with you?"

"Today, I seen Midnight murdered."

Angel looked very concerned. "What happened?"

"I was waiting in the car. He had an appointment with his PO. While I was sitting, not really paying attention, this man walks up and looks in the car as I was sitting there. After a while, I realized it was Flintstone. He looked to be about fifty years old. I don't even think he thirty yet."

"What?!"

"Yeah. He looked real bad. Angel, only if I could turn back the hands of time, this day and all the others would be so different. When Midnight walked out that door, things happened so quickly. His life slipped away so quick. The only thing I thought about was Momma. Sometimes I feel like I am going to face things on this earth the rest of my life alone." Brooklin placed her head in the palm of her hands.

"Let's go get those worries off your brain and strengthen your spirits." Angel grabbed her hand led her out the door and off to the mall they went.

Angel went to the beauty shop for the first time. Today was a special occasion. When she walked into Blue Silk, the neighborhood beauty shop, the beauticians were surprised to see her in there. She sat in Kelly's chair and got her hair spruced up with a French roll and a few Shirley Temple curls hanging in the front and along the sides. White baby's breath was placed in the top.

After leaving the beauty shop, she went to Long Nails where an Asian woman immediately asked as soon as she walked in the door, "May I help you?"

"I want a full set, pedicure, and my eyebrows waxed." Angel was instructed to go sit in the massage chair so that her pedicure could be completed. She chose the French tip design for her hands and feet. Once that was completed, she walked to the back to have her eyebrows waxed. She sat in the black leather chair and leaned her head back. The lady placed the hot wax over her eyebrow and she squeezed her eyes tightly. When the lady snatched the tape off, Angel damn near hit her. Water welled up in her eyes. She made a mental note not to ever do that again. Then it was time for the next brow. Angel lay back gripping her feet to the floor, the arms to the chair and her eyelids held tight. When the tape was snatched, she let out a loud noise.

She ran home to shower and wash her face before she headed to the Galleria Mall in Clayton. Once in the mall, she checked for the time. Her appointment was at twelve and she had ten minutes to get there. There was no time for window-shopping. In Mac, she requested Linda who let Angel know she was fine because if she had been there late, Linda would have simply waited. She knew how important this day was for her.

Linda was applying her makeup as her phone began to ring. Brooklin and Teresa were calling to find out her whereabouts. She told them she would be there as soon as she was done. Linda was done and Angel spent two hundred dollars on makeup and the accessories to apply it.

When Angel made it to the church, she went straight to the basement. Brooklin and Teresa were already dressed. They both were helping Keena with her accessories. The three of them looked like triplets wearing their sleeveless latte midriff chiffon dresses with charmeuse-rounded necklines and the sash at the waist. With hair pulled back into a ball, it reminded you of the women in the eighties from Robert Palmer's *I Didn't Mean To Turn You On* and *Simply Irresistible* videos.

Angel slid into her Vera Wang soft narrow A-line wedding gown. It tightly gathered around her breasts which created pleats in the front of the fabric that fell from the high waistline directly below the bust. All 52" of the train swept the floor.

Angel was ready to go as she had her something old something new something borrowed and something blue garter. Heading in the direction of the sanctuary, the wedding coordinator gathered the guys.

Keena met Denim as he was dressed in his cream tuxedo accented with a multi-diamond pattern Rio Latte vest and coordinating tie. Teresa followed with Brandon, and Brooklin and Ray proceeded after them.

Luther looked at his daughter wearing his

smile. She grabbed onto her father's arm and smiled back at him. She looked like the messiah he called her when he named her at birth. Tears came to her eyes as she saw her son standing as the best man looking just like his father, handsome as ever. He made his cream colored tuxedo look good. Luther informed the pastor that he was the one giving the bride away and took his seat.

"Angel, I love you and I know that God has ordained this love. On this day, I take you to be my wedded wife. Today is a very special and truly unforgettable day. It's like a dream come true. I will love and cherish you always. I recognize that God has blessed me and entrusted to me your life as a gift. Regardless of the circumstance, my purpose is to love you and to provide for your needs through the good and, if any, the bad. I want you to be my partner in life. I will forever cherish our friendship and love you faithfully through the easy and difficult. I give you this ring as I choose you to be my wife, to have and to hold from this day forward, for better or for worse, for richer or poorer, in sickness and in health, until death do we depart."

The pastor performing the service sighed out, "Wow!" The entire church laughed as he told Angel, "Girl hurry up and say your vows! This man loves you! I thought he wasn't ever going to finish!"

Angel smiled as the tears rolled down her eyes. She looked to her father and he was crying. There was no need to turn around because she could hear that Brooklin was crying. She looked to her son and he was being just the perfect gentleman. His Kodak smile brought more tears. She held her head down and cleared her throat. She reached to grab her future husband's hands as she began to speak. "This is going to simple, short and straight to the point." The congregation let out another laugh.

"Kevin, one day you asked did I know what love was. Today I am here to tell you, yes, I do know what love means." She looked him deeply into his eyes searching for his soul. "When I can no longer breathe without you and all my thoughts are constantly filled with your presence. Love is what we share. From this day forward, I will trust and honor you. I will laugh and cry with you. My love will be faithfully yours through the best and the worst of times as I have given you my hand to hold, my life to keep. So today I give you this ring. Wear it with love and joy because I have chosen you to be my husband to love you as a part of myself because in God's sight we shall be one."

Kevin kissed his bride. The church went into an uproar with cheers and hand claps. Kevin, Angel, and Lil Reggie walked over to the unity candle. Kevin lit the unity candle followed by Angel and then by Lil Reggie.

During the reception, the couple danced to K-CI and JoJo's *All My Life*. During the song, Kevin wrapped his arms around his bride and let her know he prayed for someone like her as he sang the song to her. Tears of joy filled her eyes.

Everyone looked on with joy. Then Luther stood up to dance with his daughter to Luther Vandross' *Dance With My Father*. Before the song was half way completed, Angel signaled to Brooklin so that she could dance with their father.

Angel sat with her husband, looking into the crowd as various people came and congratulated them. Reggie walked up and instantly Angel began to feel very awkward.

Angel looked him over in his thick white Stafford T-shirt, his black Evisu jeans with the white design painted on the back of his jeans, and black Prada tennis shoes. She wanted to shake her head in disgust because he couldn't change his attire not even for her wedding but he stood too close in her eyesight.

Reggie reached out to Kevin and shook his hand. "We were never formally introduced. I'm Reggie and I just wanted to say I guess the best man won. You take very good care of her 'cause if not, you have me to deal with. By the way," he looked at them both, "Congratulations." He walked away overwhelmed with hurt in his eyes before Kevin could thank him for the congratulations. He wanted to strike up a conversation to let Reggie know it wasn't about anyone winning.

Luther came over to the couple to break the ice because they now were sitting in a slump. "Where a y'all going for that honeymoon?"

Kevin smiled, "We are going to Las Vegas."

"Las Vegas? That ain't shit! I done been to Las Vegas when I was high on that crack! What about Barbados? See some islands or something? See some shit we ain't used to seeing every day."

Angel couldn't believe her father just said that. Kevin laughed as he stood up from the table to embrace Luther.

Chapter 34

NOBODY ELSE

Brooklin came back from the corner store. She was so busy laughing at Boogey and she hadn't realized that a black Hummer was following her. As she turned the corner, she attempted to look at the driver which she couldn't see due to the tinted windows. She began to do her America's Next Top Model runway walk as she strutted down the street wearing her tightly fitted green Juicy Couture jogging suit which enhanced her curves. The hood covered her head from the fall winds on the November night.

The driver window of the Hummer slowly rolled down, "Can I take you home, girl?"

Brooklin looked at this Martin Lawrence impersonator and smiled. "Thanks but no thanks." Pointing to her house that was about twelve feet from where she stood, she added, "I live right there. Maybe some other time."

"Hey, what's your name?" asked the driver.

"Brooklin," she stated with sass.

He laughed, "Brooklyn as in the BK, Brooklyn, New York?"

"Naw, Brooklin with an 'I' instead of a 'Y'," she snaked her eyes.

"Interesting, Brooklin with an 'I'. My name is June."

"June as in April, May, June, and July?" Brooklin laughed.

"You got jokes," June chuckled.

He parked his Hummer and began to walk with Brooklin. They sat on the porch and chit chatted the night away. Brooklin offered him some of her Red Hot Riplets and a swig of her Mountain Dew. He turned it down. Brooklin didn't understand his rejection. June looked like he had never missed a meal weighing a good three hundred pounds. Her qualifications didn't have any weight restrictions. He smelled and looked like new money. His diamond bezel bracelet alone lit up the street better than the street lights.

Their conversation came to a halt as Ray pulled up to drop off the twins. Ray approached the porch and Brooklin was trying to figure out why he was getting out of the car. Since Angel had moved in with Kevin, Ray would watch from the car to make sure the boys got in safely.

Ray was about to introduce himself to Brooklin's new prospect, but when she yelled "What the fuck?!," he turned his attention to what she was addressing.

A Caucasian male came running up the street with some come-fuck-me shorts on under a black jacket. He ran right up onto a porch. Brooklin figured since he was going to Mr. Whitey's house that he had to be his son or something. The house had been vacant for some years now. Mr. Whitey and his wife had died of natural causes. Ray asked when did some white people move onto their street. She told Ray and June about when they were young and they played the game nigga knocking and Mr. Whitey was on the porch standing with his strap.

"That must be his son or something. He's married to a black woman though. I have seen them coming and going lately."

June looked over at the man. "You know they do that type of shit. It can be zero below and they will be out here running around stark naked." June said his good-byes and walked to his Hummer.

Ray left without inquiring about his identity.
Two days later, Brooklin was answering her door. Standing on the other side was June wearing a black cardigan sweater with black button down under it, some black jeans she wasn't able to identify and black shiny Prada high top shoes.

"Brooklin, I didn't get your number and you didn't ask me for mine."

She stopped him before he could finish his sentence. "I knew you would be back."

June looked at his Cartier watch. "Wanna do brunch?"

Hesitantly, she answered. "My sister and I are going shopping to get Thanksgiving dinner. Can I call you later?"

"Only if I am invited for the feast." Brooklin laughed. Knowing that Ray always celebrated the holidays with them, she didn't want him to feel uncomfortable. "We will see."

June handed her the piece of paper he had already written his cell phone number on. As he walked off the porch, Angel had pulled up. She rolled down her window, ducking her head so that Brooklin could see her face, "Ask daddy if he wants to go."

"He gone already. Ray came to pick him up. He supposed to take him up to Kevin's shop and get him a haircut. They hanging out once they pick the boys up from school."

Brooklin locked the door and walked to the car. When she got in, they both watched the half-dressed individual running up to Mr. Whitey's house.

Angel laughed, "That boy must be some kin to Mr. Whitey's crazy ass. Running out here in them little bitty ass shorts. I don't give a damn about people saying white folks don't get cold. That's some bullshit."

"How is school coming along?" Brooklin asked as Angel pulled off.

"It's coming. Next semester, I will be doing a lab up at BJC hospital. When are you going to start doing something with yourself and leaving these damn duffle bag boys alone? It's like you comfortable at the bottom." Angel was making reference to June as she saw him drive away in his black Hummer.

"The only time when I am at the bottom is when I am on my back getting the shit fucked out of me. That ain't often cuz a bitch like getting hit from the back. If you are talking about June, he approached me."

"Any who, Brooklin, everybody approaches you. I don't understand why you won't get back with Ray. Nobody else is going to treat you the way he does. Even if that man is messing around with someone else, I can't tell. As much as he has his kids, they ain't never seen him with another woman."

Brooklin wasn't trying to hear it. "Angel, have you ever thought about this: maybe Ray's gay."

"Get the fuck outta here!" Angel waved her hand.

Brooklin had to laugh at herself. "I know that nigga's fucking somebody. He just ain't out in the open with it, but money makes him cum just like it does for me."

"Money makes him cum. That nigga still hustling."

"He ain't never stop. He quiet with that shit. Ray gets his work and them niggas from Beam Street move that shit. He even fucks with Reggie."

"Reggie!?" exclaimed Angel.

"Yeah Double R., Yo baby daddy, Reggie. That dude right there is caked up. He got a team of young wolves working for him."

"He bet not being doing that bullshit around my son."

Angel and Brooklin got out of the car and walked towards the entrance to Soulard Market. They were getting sweet potatoes, fresh greens and fruit from the farmers that would be selling produce dirt cheap. Leaving the market, they headed to Schnucks, a local grocery store, to get the remaining items on the list.

When they made it back to the house, Kevin, Ray and Luther were there to unload the groceries. Angel looked Ray all the way over. She wondered if Kevin knew anything about the way Ray was making his living.

Chapter 35

THAT'S WHAT I NEED

June didn't make it to the feast but he understood. It saddened him when Brooklin spoke of her mother. He couldn't believe that her childhood friend would do such a heinous crime. He also couldn't believe how she had opened up to him so quickly. All she talked about was how happy she was for her baby sister.

Sitting at a booth at Uncle Bill's Pancake House, Brooklin was approached by the waitress. "Excuse me? We are out of orange juice. Would you like something else?"

Brooklin couldn't believe that they would be out of orange juice, but it was two o'clock in the morning. Being that Uncle Bill's stayed open twenty-four hours three hundred sixty-five days of the year serving the best pancakes in the Midwest, it was understandable. She opted for sweet tea and they did have that.

When the waitress arrived to the booth with their food, Brooklin was preoccupied with Ray pulling out the chair for some chic with a big dumb ass. Brooklin thought about her and Angel's conversation about Ray a couple days before. She couldn't wait to tell Angel that she saw Ray with some girl that had a big ghetto booty.

June noticed Brooklin's look of pandemonium written all over her face. He led his eyes in the direction in which he saw her looking. "Ain't that your baby daddy, Ray?"

It never crossed Brooklin's mind not one time that she had ever told him his name as she nodded yes.

"He with that stripper chic, Passion. She strips over at the Pink Slip. She the hottest commodity they got. They should call her ass Ms. New Booty." June laughed as he put a piece of his well-done steak in his mouth.

Brooklin could barely eat her food. She stopped watching Ray and held a conversation with June. She talked freely with her thoughts wandering about in her head about Ray.

June was about to take her home. They had hung out all day. When Brooklin informed him she wasn't ready to call it a night, he drove downtown to the Riverfront. He parked at the bottom of the Arch steps. June looked up and talked about how Nelly had made this Arch so famous. Brooklin didn't care about how all his relatives wanted to see the Arch whenever they came to visit.

He could tell that Brooklin seeing Ray with that woman was heavy on her mind. It was obvious how she walked over to the table to introduce herself when June was at the cash register paying the bill. Ray hadn't seen Brooklin the entire time. He was so into his conversation that he didn't notice her walk up. The booty had him mesmerized.

June asked Brooklin did she want to get out of the car and walk the Arch grounds. She obliged. The November night air wasn't that bad. She was still dressed for the weather in her orange and blue Aeropostale jogging suit.

They made their way up the top of the Arch steps. Taking a seat near the bench that was a few steps from the Arch, they watched the cars roll by, couples strolling on the Arch grounds, the waves of the river flowing, and the gamblers loading the casino boats.

Noticing that they were the only ones close to the Arch and their presence went on unknown, June placed his Magnum on his eight inches of hard on. He had it in his pocket for just in case something popped off as it did, Brooklin couldn't believe that his fat ass was packing that much. He pulled himself out and she pulled her jogging pants down as if she was about to take a seat on the toilet. June spread his legs just enough for Brooklin to fit in between. She braced herself placing her hands on his wide thighs. She bounced up and down while grinded her hips around his lap. Brooklin watched facing the passersby and all June could see was the back of her head. With a slight lean of his back, he rose as he was about to cum. Brooklin slowed down as she reached her peak right with him. Her wetness was all over the front part of jeans. It slightly showed but he didn't care. He was going home after he dropped her off. Pulling their clothes up, they headed back to his Hummer.

June had Brooklin feeling like she was in heaven. Her darkness was behind her. She was spreading her wings and reaching for the sky. The emptiness feeling she felt when she saw Ray was gone. She hadn't even mentioned it to Angel. She knew Angel would have taken his side anyway.

She had overexposed herself to June. He took heed to every word she had spoken. Brooklin came to grips that it was Ray's prerogative to do who he wanted to do. Nobody but him, and now June, had her feeling the feeling that she was feeling. The situation between her and June was a bit shady. He had never taken her to his place of residence. As soon as she brought it to his attention, he jumped right on it. The upcoming date would be at his house.

June was becoming that someone special. He was giving up sweet love all through the night. She was willing to open up her heart and wasn't worried about him breaking it. Brooklin was feeling like he would never leave her lonely. She was able to share her ups and downs with him.

Chapter 36

ONE FOR THE MONEY

Reggie stepped out of his old school Chevy. His blue candy-paint was sitting on twenty-fours. TV's were in the headrest. His young goons knew he was supreme. They checked him out as if he was brushing the dirt off his shoulders in his usual Stafford thick white tee over his white thermal and fresh white on white Forces. His platinum chain with the diamond cross pendant spoke for itself. He stepped up to the goons acknowledging everyone but only giving Toussaint his name recognition. "What it do T-Murder?" They walked and talked, leaving the crowd he once stood in. The circumstances didn't bother anyone because they all knew that Reggie was the reason they were all eating.

When the conversation had ended, Reggie and Toussaint walked back to the goons as they still stood in their usual lamppost positions. "Y'all fools stay up." Reggie smiled getting back into his car. He just came through to let him know that he could pick the work up later and he was changing the location.

Reggie looked over and saw his burner sitting over on the seat. He couldn't believe he left it out like that! Right as he was about to pull over to pull his dashboard apart and place it in its stash spot, he saw a familiar face.

Flintstone was walking across the street without a care in the world. His first reaction was to get out, walk up to him and blast his ass in broad daylight. But he wasn't about to let history repeat itself. He knew those Clint Eastwood actions would send him right back to jail. Instead, he drove slowly watching his every move. Flintstone was on some type of mission. For the last hour, he didn't even notice he was being followed. Reggie parked right in front of the house Flintstone walked into. He sat there patiently waiting for him to come back out. Reggie thought, "If this was how I had handled the situation in the first place, I wouldn't be doing this right now."

Flintstone came out conversing with people on the block. Reggie figured that maybe since it was December, Flintstone thought the killers were Christmas shopping. Reggie parked his car and put on his black skull cap. He got out of his car with his burner in hand. Standing by the car, watching his target, he placed his burner in his back pocket. Due to all of the global warming, December weather wasn't like it was back in the day. Glad it was sixty degrees and the wind-chill factor wasn't too low, Reggie pulled his tee over the gun so it wouldn't be seen and pulled his cap down over his ears.

By the time Flintstone realized he was being followed, it was too late. Reggie had followed him onto the side of a vacant building. Flintstone was stopping to take a leak. When Reggie told him "this was for Midnight," he was just about done but he died holding his shaft in his hands. Reggie walked away slowly. He had to take his crisp white tee off because it was splattered with droplets of Flintstone's blood.

He made it back to his car. His identity went unnoticed. This went a lot different from the last time he had put in work. He was making too much money to be making such stupid moves. Reggie rolled out going to the nearest gas station. He bought himself a cigarette lighter. He pulled near his set and lit his tee shirt up. He watched as it burned. Memories of his brother and Midnight surfaced. This killing didn't thrill him as the previous ones did the pre-ejaculation filling was lost. Visions danced around in his head. The shock that was on Flintstone's face when he approached him, he could envision the same expression now.

When his cell phone rang, he became conscious of his whereabouts, realizing the shirt was burnt to a crisp and there was nothing but the black mark left on the ground. Tammy hung up and called right back. He spoke mildly and she could sense there was something wrong. Although they had been messing around for quite some time, he never made her feel like she was the only one. Most of his conversations were about Angel and how he couldn't believe that she had gone and gotten married. This was how he usually sounded when he would mention Angel. She said what she had to say and hung up.

"Angel, you wanna go to The Broadway with me tonight?" Brooklin held the phone waiting on her to answer.

"No, Brooklin, some other time. I have class in the morning and we learning how to draw blood."

The girls said their goodbyes and Brooklin got dressed for the club. She called June to let him know that she was going to The Broadway. He convinced her to go to The Loft. It was a new spot that had recently opened. He got her to change her mind by telling her that The Broadway wasn't like it used to be. Since she hadn't been out in such a long time, it didn't take much to convince her.

It was taking her such a long time to find something to wear. Her usual attire lately had been nothing but sweat suits. She wasn't about to wear jogging clothing to a new place. New place meant new people that didn't know her style. She looked over at the clock and figured she had enough time to make it to the mall and get herself something. Running outside to get into her car, she was almost thrown seeing this big booty woman walking up on Mr. Whitey's porch. When the ambulance came, she wanted to stop and be nosey. She saw them rush into Mr. Whitey's house as well so she knew she could find out the details later.

Walking into The Loft, Brooklin walked around looking to see if she saw any familiar faces. The crowd appeared to be a bit younger than her with a mixture of the working class. It was right by Harris-Stowe State College so she figured there must be a lot of college students in the place. The music wasn't loud. The casual conversations were hovering over the music. This place was solely for drinking. Besides the big round bar in the front of the club, there were four small ones off to the sides. Glasses were clinking louder than the music being played. The dance floor was in the back along with the DJ. You would be sure to get your drink on before you even danced.

As Brooklin walked back to do another walk around to show off that she had an apple bottom in her Apple Bottom blue jean skirt and red and gold Apple Bottom blouse, she was stopped in her tracks.

"You got to be tired because you've been running across my mind all day!" this corny individual sang. Brooklin was giving him the time a day because she could smell money.

He wore a plain brown Hollister T-shirt and some Hollister jeans. The Gucci shoes said it all but with all the knockoff stuff running around, no one could ever tell. He was toned down with a low Caesar cut and the pleasurable fragrance of Aramis Life filled the air. When she checked him out, he was wearing the Presidential Rolex. She hadn't seen too many people wearing one. Ray's was the only one she had come into contact with.

"You know you look like…"

"Don Cheadle. Everybody tells me that."
They both shared a laugh. Brooklin was laughing for different reasons. She laughed thinking about how she used to wish he was her man after seeing the movie "Colors."

"You know you are a sight for sore eyes. What they call it nowadays? Eye candy?"

"Eye candy? That's a lot better than the corny line you just hit me with."

"Speaking of eye candy, have you heard of the contest that they do over at Taylor Made?"

"I heard something about it but I ain't never inquired about it," Brooklin blushed.
"They having an Eye Candy contest. The winner gets twenty-five grand and a modeling contract."
The sound of money had Brooklin creaming as she asked, "What 's in it for you?"

"Nothing."

"I can't believe that. You just walk up to me, offer me a deal that I'm not about to refuse and I'm supposed to believe there's nothing in it for you. What I look like?" Brooklin waited on him to answer.

"Like I said, you look like some eye candy. This coming up weekend, they are having auditions. I'll see you then if you are interested."

Reggie walked up to the two. He reached out to embrace Brooklin and she welcomed the embrace. "Who's ya friend?"

Brooklin looked at him because she didn't know his name, "This is my friend…"

"Robert. Robert Taylor." He reached out to grab Reggie's hand. Reggie's right hand met Robert's right hand.
"Robert, this is my brother-in-law."

"Brother-in-law as in husband or in sister."
They all shared a laugh because it was so evident that Robert was flirting.

"As in sister my sister is married to him," Brooklin smiled.
Reggie's entourage was coming in their direction.

"I see you have a goon squad all over again." Brooklin pointed her head in his entourage's direction.

Robert said his goodbyes, letting Brooklin know that he would be looking for her before he walked away.

"Look like you hit the jackpot this time." Reggie waved for the waitress, "What ya drinking?"

"Grey Goose with cranberry. Why I hit the jackpot?" Brooklin stood next to Reggie, watching Robert walk away.

"You don't know who that is?"

Knowing she smelled money, she didn't smell the jackpot. "No! Who is it?"

"That nigga is the son of the Donald Trump of the Lou. His daddy and his people own clubs, the only black owned bank in the Lou, apartment complexes, they promote concerts, and they are in the process of buying a broadcasting network of some sort. They in some illegal shit but nobody can prove it. That family got they hands in too much legit stuff. Their distant cousin was the mayor years ago. They were rubbing elbows with the right people. Right now, the old man is looking to promote a model. Each month he was going to have things like Ms. January, Ms. February, and so on and so forth. Each month the winner wins fifteen hundred dollars. In the end, the overall winner wins twenty-five grand plus a modeling contract."

Brooklin took it all in and she knew that Saturday she had a date. She could now tell her sister she wouldn't be at the bottom for long. Modeling had never crossed her mind. But the future for it was looking bright. She finished her drink, followed by a couple more before she called it a night.

Chapter 37

ALL THAT I CAN SAY

"You know a place that people are dying to see?"

"No?" the driver of the Hummer answered.

"The cemetery." Brooklin pointed to the cemetery. "Turn in there."

The driver did as instructed but was wondering why were they in the cemetery at one in the morning. She directed him to where he needed to be. She had made the trip so much to talk to her mother she could get to the gravesite with her eyes closed. Once there, she got out of the truck before walking to the tree that was inches away from the tombstone that read "Beloved Mother."

Brooklin began to talk through her slurred speech. She was filling her mother in on the latest events. She had won Ms. Eye Candy for the month of January. She only had six more months before it was all over. Brooklin wasn't 100 percent sure she would land that modeling contract because she had some competition. Every beautiful lady in St. Louis was coming to this event.

The best thing about it was that your birth certificate had to state that you were born in

Missouri. She laughed telling her mother that the judges was telling her with a name like Brooklin it meant she wasn't from the Show-Me-State. She laughed telling her mother how she cracked their faces when she brought in her birth certificate. She let her know that she was up against a lot of beautiful young girls. She laughed thanking her mother for her beauty and her youthful look. Her driver had joined her by now; he walked over and held his hand out so that Brooklin could get her nose dirty with the dog food. She sniffed the heroin right out of his hand and before she knew it, he had her on top of her mother's tombstone with his shaft all up in her wetness.

Brooklin was reaching her climax as she screamed out, "Robert, hold me. I'm about to cum!"

If it was possible for someone to turn over in their grave, ole Tenda Brenda was flipping. Not only had her daughter had sex right there, she had gotten high right before the sex act.

"Brooklin, why is Reggie calling you so much?" Luther followed behind his daughter noticing the change she had made from the night she came home talking about being a model. He knew the change all too well, but he just wasn't sure. He talked to Angel about it. She was so wrapped up in school and work that she didn't spend all the time with her sister like she used to. Her free time was spent with Kevin and her son.

"Daddy, I don't know why he's calling! He's probably trying to get in touch with Ray." Brooklin slammed the bathroom door in Luther's face.

Talking to the bathroom door, he said, "Brooklin, something not right. The twins and I barely see you. When you here, you are sleep and then you go to the bathroom and stay for hours. Brooklin, you not doing any drugs are you?"

Brooklin sat on the toilet and looked at the door. She stood up to look in the mirror. Her appearance hadn't changed. She stood on the scale. She still weighed 145. So she tried to figure out what made her father say that.

"Daddy, do you believe in God?"

"Yes, I believe. If it wasn't for Him, I wouldn't be able to stand here as healthy as I am today!" Luther silently thanked Him for his well-being. "But what that got to do with you?"

"Well, you should believe in me! Believe that I'm okay."

Luther knew something was wrong. How his daughter could be comparing herself to the Almighty?!

"Now girl don't talk with such foolishness. You don't know the powers that Man has. Now you hush with that foolishness." Luther spoke with his most sincere voice.

Brooklin thought about the situation and knew that this wasn't the right time for her motive. She reassured Luther that she was okay. She opened the door so he could see she was there doing the number two. He waved the smell and walked away.

After leaving the funk, Luther called for Brooklin. Someone was at the door. When she made it to the door, she was so surprised to see June. She walked outside and they sat on the porch. As they talked about her being so busy that he hadn't seen her in so long, she thought about how she was beginning to feel like he was her everything. With the mentioning of money, she forgot all about the closure she was contemplating on him bringing to her life.

June let her know that he had seen her in all the local papers as one of the EYE CANDY candidates. When he told her she had to be the oldest one in that contest, it brought her spirits down.

Although she was approaching thirty, she didn't look a day over twenty-one. He knew it as well as she did. She brought the conversation to an end. She asked him was his number the same and let him know she would call him later.

Once she made it back in, the phone rang. She answered. It was Reggie telling her to meet him at Fairgrounds. Brooklin wanted to know what was so important but she agreed to meet him.

When Brooklin arrived at the park, she drove around looking for Double R. She couldn't believe he was still on the earth breathing from all the shit he and his friends had been through. She was getting upset that she couldn't find him. That put her in a state of mental conflict. After circling the park several times, she found R near the basketball court.

Reggie stopped bouncing the ball and walked over to the bench to take a seat. "Hey Ms. Eye Candy!"

Brooklin could hear the sarcasm in his voice. She walked over to the bench and took a seat next to him. "What you call me out here for?"

"I'm about to make you an offer you can't refuse."

"Alright movie mogul, tell me what you really called me out here for. If this has something to do with my sister, you can count me out of it. Cinderella is living happily ever after."

Reggie looked at Brooklin as if he couldn't believe she said that to him. "This has nothing to do with Angel. This has everything to do with you." He bounced the basketball waiting on her to ask another question.

Brooklin watched the cars roll by. She couldn't believe that they were the only ones in the park right now. It wasn't all that hot although it was almost the end of June.

Reggie began to talk. "This fellow by the name of Greg is having some problems. He is getting too much heat. He can't make his usual moves. This is causing problems for me and Ray."

"You and Ray ass need to work this out. This ain't got shit to do with me."

"It does. Just let me finish. Greg and this dude came up together. His friend ventured off into some legitimate ventures, but he stills gets his hands dirty. Greg knows a lot of this man's personal business. Now Greg's boss wants him to handle the situation because this guy is trying to get bigger than the boss and they want him to stay in his place."

"Enough with the Colombo and Perry Mason shit. What I got to do with this?" Brooklin was getting tired of hearing the story.

"Brooklin, do you believe that you have a chance with a modeling career?"

"Why wouldn't I?"

"Your age for one. Have you paid attention to your competition? Those other girls range from 18-25."

That very moment, Brooklin didn't believe in herself. Twice today there was mention of her age.

Reggie continued. "We are not asking you to risk your life. We just want you to keep your little boyfriend in the club after hours. You can walk away with a lot of money. Everybody knows he gets his nose dirty, so your job will be so easy."

"Why go in the club? Why don't you hit the bank?"

"I'm not about to do no bank. I have to admit that's way out of my league. That shit is insured. Besides, this man has money hidden in all of his businesses. I'm talking about large amounts. He has had safes built that are durable to fires. He keeps the majority of his money at the Taylor Made joint."

"How much money we talking about?" Brooklin was about to see if pursing the modeling was worth giving up.

"It shouldn't be less than three million." Reggie spoke with confidence.

"Get the fuck outta here! I'm supposed to believe that bullshit?! That man got over three million dollars in that club?!"

"Over two million." Reggie wanted to laugh because that's how he felt when the conversation was brought to him, "Do you believe in God?"

"Now don't start with that mess. To answer your question, I do believe in God because He was the only one that got me out of the Jerk house."

"Brooklin, all I have to say is we got our plan together. On Sunday, they are having their annual Player's Ball and every day after that, something is going down. Martini Monday, Two Dollar Tuesday, Wet-n-Wild Wednesday, Throwback Thursday, Fight Friday. And you know that's going to be big because that Spinks fight is going to be Friday instead of Saturday. So on Saturday after the July Eye Candy contest, it should pop off."

"You know where everything at?"

"All the bases have been covered. You just need to keep daddy's lil boy occupied there after hours."

"What about his daddy? You not going to do nothing to him?"

"His daddy will be taken care of. That weekend happens to be his anniversary. After the fight Friday, he and his wife have a flight that leaves for Acapulco first thing Saturday morning. And you don't have to worry about your boyfriend. You just make sure that he get himself so high that he almost falls into a comatose state." Reggie laughed and bounced the basketball.

That was Ray's cue to approach. He walked up and spoke to Brooklin. He let her know that she would not be implicated in any shape, form, or fashion. He went on to tell that he would never put her in harm's way. She believed him and at that moment she knew everything was going to be okay.

She gathered herself and began to walk away. It was still a bit unbelievable. "You never told me how much I was getting out of this."

Ray looked at her and she was as beautiful as the first day they met. "Instead of twenty-five grand how does a million sound?"

When Brooklin got in her car, she was trying to think how much was a million. Where would she put it? How could she hide that? She drove off.

"Man what if all that money is not there?" Reggie asked Ray.

"Look man, whatever is there, it's ours. We don't have to give it to nobody. The plan is we hit the man's pockets. So whatever is there we can have. This is not Fort Knox. Nothing is guarded. The man can't report it. He keeps money at his spots so he don't have to pay taxes on it. You want out the game and I won't out of this. This is an early retirement. Nobody has never robbed this man. People don't even know how he moves. This man need to know you can't hide the money in the cookie jar anymore. You need to guard it at all times. This gonna be just like taking candy from a baby. What you 'bout to do?" Ray waited on Reggie to answer.

"I ain't 'bout to do nothing. Probably bend a couple of corners. Then lay it down. I'm going to meet up with T-Murder and let him know I need him and his goon squad to carry a couple of duffle bags." Reggie doubted that it was going to be that easy. Get in the office, roll up a rug, and hit the jackpot. Now that was some eye candy he wanted to see. It's not very often that the bad guy gets away. He was so lost in his thoughts, he barely paid attention to Ray.

"Do that. Passion waiting on me. I'm 'bout see if I can get her to do something strange for a little change."

"Nigga that's her job. She always doing something for some change." Reggie laughed at his comment.

"Aye Double R," Ray called out.

"What?" he turned to face Ray.

"I can respect that thug in you. As close as we came, you never let me know that was you that stole that product from Rance back in the day."

Reggie turned without making a comment. If Ray thought he was about to confess, he misjudged that whole situation. He would never admit to all the wrong he had committed. His thoughts was this nigga got to be dumb thinking I'm 'bout to converse about his dirt that went deeper than the sea.

Ray met up with Passion. She met him at the Royal Palace. It wasn't too far from Fairgrounds. She had fallen in love with the shrimp. Ray sat there admiring Passion. He just now believed that he could love someone other than Brooklin. At this very hour, he told Passion all that there was to tell. She took a special interest in the death of Brooklin's mother. She had lost her own mother to Lupus. At the time, the illness went unknown; her mother was unable to care for her children. They were both separated and sent away after they moved to St. Louis.

Chapter 38

FIRE AND DESIRE

Luther got into Kevin's truck with Angel. "You know I have never been to Six Flags. I can't believe I let you talk me into this."

"Well, daddy, you only live once." Angel looked over at her dad. Her hair was pulled back in a ponytail and she was flossing in her stunna shades.

"I talked to Harlem this morning. We talked for a long time. Him and his wife are doing just fine. He's convinced himself he has nothing here worth coming back." Luther gazed out the window, wishing his only son would give him that second chance his girls had given him.

"Well, daddy, that's your child. I gave up trying to figure him out a long time ago. I used to try to impress him, but then I thought about it. He had never did anything to impress me. He never told me thanks for the money I gave him to apply to those colleges he was interested in. But I don't even want to talk about that in front of the boys."

Brooklin walked out of her front door. She was about to get in her car when she noticed Passion coming from out of Mr. Whitey's house. The temptation in being nosey had her wondering why the mystery lady that was with her baby daddy at Uncle Bill's was now across the street from her. With her interest enticed, instead of getting into her car, she crossed the street.

"Excuse me. Is everything okay over there? I noticed the ambulance was here the other day."

"Yeah everything is everything. My co-worker suffered a minor heart attack. He's fine. I was coming to see if his wife needed anything." Passion moved closer to Brooklin.

A casual conversation was brought up. Brooklin wanted to ask her where did she know Ray from but she thought different about that. She didn't want her to think that was the sole purpose of coming across the street. She actually wanted to know about the new family on the block. Passion didn't know that Brooklin was the Block Captain in her own warped mind.

Taylor Made was packed. All of the previous months' Eye Candy winners were there. All accept one. Robert was looking for Brooklin. When he last spoke to her, she was on her way out the door. It shouldn't have taken her no more than forty-five minutes to make it there. When show time came and Ms. July was selected, Robert figured that something came up with Brooklin. He never tried to call to see if she was okay. He had his eyes on some new eye candy that he planned on getting a taste of after hours.

Angel pulled up in front of Tolliver's so that Luther could get himself some beer. Six Flags had worn him out. Boogey was there in his usual spot.

"Hey Salt!" Boogey waved to Angel.

Angel rolled her window so that she could hear

him clearer.

"I haven't seen you in a long time. This must be my night. I didn't see you together but to see you both in one night is some exquisite stuff. Pepa just not too long ago left. She was riding with someone. That chic I hear she be stripping and stuff," Boogey informed her.

Luther made it back to the truck. "What his drunk ass putting on about?"

"Nothing. He just seen Brooklin with some stripper girl," Angel waved her hand and pulled off.

Pulling up in front of the house, Luther opened the door to go inside his home. "You boys coming with Grams?"

Without answering, they told their good-byes to Angel and exited the truck with their PSPs and Six Flags paraphernalia. Luther had really bonded with the boys. He was giving them something he stopped providing for his children. Although he missed Harlem's presence, his three grandsons filled that void.

As Robert secured the doors to the club, he noticed that some patrons were still dwelling around the parking lot. This wasn't out of the norm because usually after the club closed, individuals would be outside putting on a car show or looking to take something hot home for the night. Right as he was walking away he heard a knock on the glass. He turned around to see this clean cut fellow wearing his tan pants and a tan jacket. He could see that he was saying something but he couldn't make it out. It was merely due to the fact that glass windows to the club were bulletproof. Robert got closer to the door and could hear the fellow saying something about some keys.

"Ms. July, look over there and see if you see some keys."

This half-dressed J-Lo look-a-like looked around until she found some keys lying near the bar. She walked towards the keys; as she reached for them, she yelled out, "Here they are!"

Robert went to open the door so that the individual could walk in to retrieve their keys. Everything that he stood for fell. Tonight, he thought it was rock-a-bye baby when he was looking down the barrel of the three eighty. Robert had underestimated Ray's appearance.

Robert took a bow. "My last curtain call." He had snorted him some dope so the seriousness of the situation had dawned on him.

Reggie's goon squad trotted into the club. Reggie took his time as he approached the door. He was feeling that situation of the two little men on his shoulders talking to him. He paused and thought about how all his life he's had the upper hand on his victim. He knew nothing about this victim, but another individual wanted his spot. He was feeling like Biggie but he had been in this shit since '90 instead of '92. He loved to bust but he wasn't ready to die. He had grabbed his gat and called his clique. Doing this shit over a decade, he had been through a lot of shit. This situation was a tight one, but his options weren't to fight or run. He would walk away. That night, Reggie walked away with a clear conscious. He had lost his brother and some of his closest friends and right now he was the only one that was left to reminisce on the good and bad times.

This morning, the thought of getting over a million dollars was cool. In and out and taking candy from a baby was too good to be true. He dodged and ducked bullets all his life. He no longer had to do this. Double R thought about what would happen if somebody walked away with his stash.

He got in his car and rode out. He pulled up to the White Castle that wasn't too far from the club. Just as he was about to place his order, the sounds of a fire truck drowned the sound coming out of the speaker. Once it was over, he was able to place his order.

Reggie drove through his neighborhood and he could envision Richard, Scary, Lay-Loc, and Midnight standing there. He continued his drive and listened to the music. DOC's "Let the Bass Go" flared through the speakers as he bobbed his head and thought about when he first was on the phone with Angel and she was listening to her rap music.

He made it home. He was surprised that his phone hadn't rung one bit knowing that Ray should have been pissed that he didn't follow in behind the little goon squad.

When the morning arrived, Reggie stretched, grabbed his remote and turned the television on. The news reporter was standing in what used to be the club Taylor Made. "That's some cold shit!"

The news reporter informed its viewers that the perpetrators were there to rob the place. They knew exactly where the money was at. With the money generated from this week's events, it was believed to be over four hundred million dollars. The reporter placed an emphasis that the thieves weren't aware that the wheel on the safe was turned to the left instead of the right, causing a five minute delay before everything around the safe would ignite all of its surroundings. The contents in the safe would be the only thing to survive the flames and the water from the sprinkler system. The one victim that was able to escape suffered with third degree burns. He was in a local hospital in critical condition.

Reggie figured that Robert would have been the only one there to know that so he must have been the one to survive out of the other six that was found.

Chapter 39

IT'S GOING DOWN

Brooklin looked around. This place was so familiar. How she got there was the question. Passion walked from the kitchen with a bowl in her hand. She was eating some white grapes.

"You just missed the news, Ms. Eye Candy. It's a good thing that you didn't make it to the club. You would have burned down with it."

Brooklin felt real sluggish. All she could remember is firing up a blunt with the individual who was telling her it was a good thing she didn't make it to the club. She had been high before, but this feeling had her body numb. She noticed that she was at her old place of residence. A sense of security started to set in. Eventually Ray would walk through the door. So she thought. Thoughts of his little girlfriend losing this battle spread like wild fire in her mind. But she continued to blame herself for being in this situation. She just wanted to ease her state of mind knowing who her new neighbors were.

As soon as Luther saw the news, he phoned Angel. He let her know that Brooklin hadn't come home and it was so unusual for her not to call to let him know she wasn't coming. Since they stayed at the house together, she always made her father aware of the all-nighters she would pull.

Angel let him know that she would call around to the jails and the hospitals. Right when she was about to make that call, it dawned on her that Boogey had seen who Brooklin was with. She called her father back to lay the information on him. When her father made it clear that being with another female other than her was out the norm, she called Kevin at work to find out if he knew something about the victims that were found burned at the club.

They could only be identified by their dental records. She was surprised to find out that Ray was the one who survived. Angel began to wonder why he was even at that club, but he wasn't the factor. Brooklin was her only concern.

"Brooklin. BK. Are you as tough as that borough you were named after? Of course not. You wouldn't be high on that PCP like you are." Passion walked back and forth in front of Brooklin while she sat on the couch. Passion placed her hands behind her back. With a demonic look in her eyes and an angelic smile, she said, "You don't even know who I am. But let me introduce myself. I am Veronica Jackson. I'm here in St. Louis by the way of Decatur, IL. My job is with the Federal Bureau of Investigations. I was placed on assignment. This kingpin by the name of Greg had a guy by the name of Carlos snitch on him. So in return they gave us Ray. If it wasn't for him trying to get a taste of this monkey, you wouldn't be sitting here in this situation. See my brother had told me all about this girl he was so in love with. Once he mentioned your name, with a name like Brooklin in a city like St. Louis, I wouldn't be able to forget that." Passion pulled a chair right in front of Brooklin and continued, "Now Ray's talkative ass told me how my brother took your mother's life. I'm convinced that you provoked him. Just so you know my brother was all I had."

Brooklin gathered her thoughts. "Why would you bring me here of all places? If you are planning to do something to me, torture me or anything, I am going to be found." Brooklin's head slumped into her chest. The drug had her drained. Not holding her head up, she asked, "Veronica, do you believe in me?"

She laughed, "I believe you are not going to make it out of here alive. I have been missing. My comrades are worried about me. Once they come looking for me, getting rid of you is going to be a piece of cake. I am going to fake like you held me against my own will. In some jealous baby momma rage, you pull out a weapon, but instead of me getting hurt, you die. Then my brother can rest in peace."

Angel had always told Brooklin she gets herself caught up in some mess, but this mess was unbelievable. Although she was sitting in the situation, it was so unrealistic to her.

Passion walked towards the back of the house. Brooklin could hear someone fumbling with the lock. Her vision was blurred but she could see a figure entering the room. He was dressed in his FBI attire; she could make out the bold yellow lettering on the hat. She also saw that he had his weapon in his hand.

Passion left the window. She was getting impatient waiting on Ray to come. She knew he was being tailed so her plan would work out fine. The figure went into the side room that was to the left of the couch.

Brooklin yelled, "Can you bring me a glass of milk?"

Passion brought the glass of milk with no hesitation. Brooklin asked for more until she drunk the whole gallon. Passion never questioned her about why choosing milk for a beverage.

When Passion walked back towards the entrance left of the couch, in seconds she heard the sound of the taser. She instantly hit the floor. The agent reached near her neck to feel for her pulse. It was still there.

Brooklin looked at the agent. "June! What are you doing here?"

"My job, Brooklin."

In moments, the house was flooded with agents. They ransacked Ray's house and found nothing. Brooklin was questioned about his whereabouts but she had no clue.

When the ambulance arrived on the scene, she was checked out. She refused hospital treatment. Once she signed the form stating she denied services, Agent DeMarco Wilson escorted her home.

When she arrived home, Luther was at the door. He was pacing back and forth. Every car that drove up put him on the porch. When he saw his child being escorted by the agent, he looked like a deer caught by some headlights.

"Brooklin, where have you been?" Luther waited on his daughter to answer.

"You wouldn't believe me if I told you!" Brooklin thought about the recent events.

"I was worried. I found out Ray was in the hospital and I ran over there to see him. He was in critical condition. He was coming to look for you at the club when I told him I couldn't find you. When he was about to enter the club, it caught fire and he ran back out."

Brooklin looked at Luther with a strange look. She noticed they were walking past Ray's car. She was trying to figure out why his car was in front of her house and he wasn't with it. Then it hit her that whatever Luther wasn't saying in front of June was worth waiting to find out.

As Brooklin entered her home, the feeling of being safe and secure shadowed her. It was time to do some re-evaluation. She was no longer about to be at the bottom. Ray loved her like a good man ought to. Playing with one emotion put her in an unbelievable situation. She didn't know why she did the things she did but she knew that this one piece of eye candy was getting too old to keep playing childish games. After feeling half past dead, it was time to take the load off and with Ray is where she would be. Now Angel wouldn't be the only one living like Cinderella. She knew with Ray is where her loyalty needed to remain.

www.ingramcontent.com/pod-product-compliance
Lightning Source LLC
Chambersburg PA
CBHW072220170626
46813CB00003B/1023